Boss'N Up 3:
Never, Ever, Fold

Royal Nicole

Lock Down Publications & Ca$h Presents
Boss'N Up 3

Boss'N Up 3

Lock Down Publications
P.O. Box 1482
Pine Lake, Ga 30072-1482

Visit our website at **www.lockdownpublications.com**

Copyright 2017 Boss'n Up 3

First Edition May 2017
Printed in the United States of America
*This is a work of fiction. Names, characters, places, and
incidents either are products of the author's imagination or
are used fictitiously. Any similarity to actual events or
locales or persons, living or dead, is entirely coincidental.*

Cover design and layout by: Dynasty's Cover Me
Book interior design by: Shawn Walker
Edited by: Mia Rucker

Stay Connected with Us!

Text **LOCKDOWN** to 22828 to stay up-to-date with new releases, sneak peaks, contests and more…

Thank you!

Submission Guideline.

Submit the first three chapters of your completed manuscript
to ldpsubmissions@gmail.com, subject line: Your book's title.
The manuscript must be in a .doc file and sent as an attachment.
Document should be in Times New Roman, double spaced and in
size 12 font. Also, provide your synopsis and full contact information. If sending multiple submissions, they must each be in a
separate email.

Have a story but no way to send it electronically? You can still
submit to LDP/Ca$h Presents. Send in the first three chapters,
written or typed, of your completed manuscript to:

LDP: Submissions Dept
Po Box 1482
Pine Lake, Ga 30072

DO NOT send original manuscript. Must be a duplicate.

Provide your synopsis and a cover letter containing your full
contact information.

Thanks for considering LDP and Ca$h Presents.

Chapter 1

Yaseer opened his eyes and looked around at his surroundings. He looked to his left and saw Kai'yan getting up off of the floor. Then he looked to his right and saw Liam, London, and Zyon with their tools aimed at Jillian, who looked as though someone had rushed her to the couch. The side of his cheekbone stung a little from being grazed by the bullet, but right then he didn't even care about that. He was beyond vexed and more than ready to send her to meet her maker. He needed to get his daughters first, then he would send Jillian's soul off with pleasure.

"Grab her, get her secured, and let's go. I ain't even about to play with this dumb bitch," Yaseer said to the crew as he got up off of the floor and brushed himself off. This was one of the main reasons he was ready to let this life go. He was tired of putting his and his family's lives at risk. He was beginning to realize it wasn't worth it. At first, it was to get money to survive, now they each had more than enough to live off of for the rest of their lives as long as they used their money correctly. Yaseer made a vow to himself that once he got his daughters back, then he would be done. He was going to wrap up this last business deal, then get the hell on through. Yaseer walked up the stairs to the DJ booth and grabbed the mic.

"I wanna thank y'all for coming out tonight. I know I be working y'all hard, but what's the fun in working with no play? Now that we got the bullshit out the way, we got plenty of drinks to go around and it's on the house. The DJ is hot, so as my boy Kevin Hart would say, Turn Up! Oh yea, when the club close tonight, y'all can take the rest of the night off, but I expect to see y'all back on the grind in the a.m., understood?"

"Yeah!" he heard a few dudes shout out, along with head nods in the crowd. Yaseer handed the mic back to the DJ and made his way down the black spiral staircase. Then he nodded at his crew, signaling them to come on. They all left out, piled up in their cars, and were ready to go put in work.

Yaseer was the first to pull up at the Chambers. He lit a blunt and rested his head on the headrest of his seat for a split second before hopping out of the car. He walked over to the door and posted up as the crew parked. He had so much on his brain. He couldn't wait til this was over. He missed his daughters and he missed his fiancé. He had yet to spend time with his newborn sons, Yaseer Jr. and Jaseer. Now that he had Adela's real name and information, he had been able to broaden his search for his daughters. If everything panned out correctly, he would have them in his arms tonight. He was just waiting to receive a phone call from his mans. So right then, he was ready to send this chick, well his cousin, Jillian, to meet her maker. He nodded his head at Kai'yan, Zyon, Liam, and London as they got out of the car. They all walked to the trunk of Kai'yan's blacked out Yukon XL, popped the trunk, and pulled out a tied up Jillian.

Yaseer could feel the hatred building in his heart just thinking about this lady even laying her hand on his seeds because he aborted her fucked up seed. In his head, it was something she should've done to avoid having a bitch ass nigga for a son. Yaseer turned and put the code in to get inside of the Chambers. He already knew what he wanted to do to her. A smile crept on his face. He was going to thoroughly enjoy this, he actually couldn't wait. Yaseer held the door open for his crew so that they could bring their next victim in for play time. Once they were all in the establishment, he let the door shut and lock, then led the way to the special room that he planned on using.

Yaseer stopped in front of a black door that had a gold number seven engraved in it. He pulled out his keychain and used his master key to unlock the door. Once more, he held the door open for his crew to enter. Upon entry, it looked like a beautiful and elegantly decorated bathroom with its granite counter tops and warmed tiles. There were gold lined the black sinks, along with black and gold decorations, throughout the bathroom. It was very spacious, spacious enough to have a garden style tub with Jacuzzi jets in it, as well as a stand-up shower. But instead of glass shower doors, it had plastic showers doors that were made out of nothing but organic plastic.

Yaseer rubbed his hands in anticipation of what was about to go down. He was more than ready. He wasn't even in the mood to question her. He was just ready to give her that long slow death that he had been waiting to give her since everything had happened with the twins getting kidnapped and him finding out that she was the one behind it. She had messed with the wrong G. Did she not realize that he and his crew were the *Heart of the Streetz*? Nobody did anything to any of them and just simply got away. They didn't play that. Yaseer was about to give her a lesson on who they really were and show her that *The Torture Crew* truly lived up to their name. He didn't even need her to tell him where his daughters were, he already had his street connects on it, and they always came through with finding any and every one that Yaseer needed found, which was why he always broke them off properly in advance, knowing they would show results. Failure was not an option.

"Get her chained," Yaseer ordered as he took off his bulletproof vest as well as his tools. Then he pulled his THT chain off followed by his crisp black T. Yaseer stood, leaning back on the counter of the sink with his arms crossed, watching his crew chain Jillian inside the shower, laced in nothing but a black wife beater that fit him to perfection, some black sweats that sagged a little, showing off the top his black briefs, topped off with his classic black timbs. He ran a hand over his fresh Caesar cut, leaned up off the sink, walked inside of the stand-up shower, and stood face to face with Jillian. He was about to open his mouth to say something to her but was paused when his phone started vibrating in his pocket. Yaseer pulled out his Galaxy S5 and had to hold in his grin when he saw it was his street connects calling. He swiped his thumb across the screen to accept the call.

"You got 'em?" was the greeting his caller received.

"Yea, we got 'em," they replied.

"A'ight, stay put, we'll be there in 45," Yaseer replied, then disconnected the call.

A smile crept over his face. He was happier than a gay man at the gay pride parade. He looked at Jillian with his arms folded across his chest, showing off the partial sleeve of artwork on his left upper arm, as well as some artwork on his chest. Just looking at her, it took everything within him not to beat the shit out of her. She had messed with his seeds and now she was about to pay with her life in the worst way. Her hands were pulled over her head, chained to a chain that was bolted to the ceiling. The shower itself was made out of nothing but organic plastic, including the shower head. That was the only way that shower could be made. Nothing else could hold what was about to come through the special pipes and into the shower. Her feet were held together by organic plastic strips that were made to hold onto just about anything, similar to the yellow strips of plastic that held stacks of phone books together.

"Did you really think I wouldn't get my daughters back? You would have been better off just aiming to kill me. Hell, you was at my house every day. You had access to all my foods and drinks, you could've simply poisoned me, but nnnaaaww, you had to go all out of the box, trying to give me a fate worse than death by attempting to take away the ones that I love the most."

Yaseer shook his head, tucked his bottom lip in his mouth, and semi turned so that she could not see the emotion laced throughout his face. Then he turned around swiftly, letting the back of his right hand lead the way to her face. All the anger that he had pent up in him landed right on the side of Jillian's face. Yaseer grasped her by her jaw and brought her face up to look at him.

"If your son couldn't even defeat me and my team, what the hell made you thought you would do it better? What you mad for? Cause I murked his punk ass. Hell, I did you and the world a favor. He was polluting the earth, and the last thing earth needs is anymore sorry ass bastards polluting its realm."

Yaseer let her jaw lose then turned to London. "Aye, L, come handle this light work for me," he spat as he stepped out of the shower. He wanted so badly to beat the breaks off of shawty, but he was raised to never put his hands on a female. He had let his anger get the best of him when he hit Jillian, but he refused to lose control and let it happen again. He was actually glad that London had showed up because now he had someone who could beat the breaks off of shawty before he sent her to hell, where she belonged.

London nodded her head and walked past him, happy to handle his light work for him. This bitch had hit her man over the head, then almost got his life ended, then turned around and kidnapped her nieces and tried to kill her girl! London was more than ready to put in overtime on Jillian. London pulled her 9mm from her gun holster on the side. She gripped it tightly. Her blood was boiling just thinking about everything Jillian had done. She turned the butt of the gun upwards. She bent slightly so that she could look in Jillian's face, who had her head bent down.

"Aye, hoe, look up, bitch." Jillian raised her eyes instead of her head, looking as if she would rip London's head off if she could get to her.

"Yea, bitch, that's right, look at me. You see, I'm the one you should've came for 'cause I'm about to be your worst fuckin' nightmare and you ain't even sleep yet. You like hitting mofos with guns. Umm K, I got something foe yo little petty ass." With those last words, London lifted the butt of her gun and commenced to whooping Jillian. All London could see was the faces of everyone that Jillian and Ezra had tried to hurt and kill. Jillian screamed out in agony as London went in on her like she was trying to take her life right then and there.

"London! London! Hey! Hey! I said that's enough!" Yaseer yelled, getting more upset by the second because London was so in the zone that she couldn't even hear him.

"Liam, get her." Liam was already moving before Yaseer could finish his request. He shook his head. Seeing her go in on ole girl made him think twice about ever getting on her bad side. Just as London had raised the butt of the gun to hit Jillian once more, Liam grabbed her wrist tightly.

"Yo, ma, chill."

London looked back at Liam with tears in her eyes. Her chest was heaving up and down in anger. This woman and her sons had tried to take away the people she loved, her family, something her and Paris didn't really have as they were growing up. Liam used his other hand to hold on to her waist and pull her back towards his chest while his other hand that held her wrist slowly made its way to her hand and eased the gun out of it. He held on to her tightly as he guided her out of the shower.

"Seer, I'ma take her out to get her calmed down," Liam said to Yaseer as he led London to the door. Yaseer nodded his head in understanding. Once Liam and London were out of the room, Yaseer gave the next order.

"A'ight, come on y'all, let's strip this bitch." Yaseer, Kai'yan, and Zyon took their blades out and walked over to the shower. They stepped inside and slit the side of her shirt and pants. Then they ripped them clean off her body and proceeded to do the same to her under garments. Once she was completely naked, they stepped out and closed the shower door. Yaseer double checked it to make sure it was secured before taking the remote out of a hidden spot in the cabinet beside the shower.

"Enjoy ya shower, doll," Yaseer spat as he walked towards the door. "Oh, and I want lights out," Yaseer said over his shoulder as he grabbed the door handle and pressed a button on the remote causing the shower to start. Yaseer smiled sinisterly as Jillian screamed at the top of her lungs for dear life as her body was being cleaned off by hydrofluoric acid. He walked out with the smile still plastered on his face.

"Call them boys and tell them to come get this bitch's remains, and tell them to make sure they use PPE (Personal Protective Equipment) and use special care while getting her out so they don't get burnt."

Royal Nicole

Chapter 2

"You good, L?" Yaseer questioned London.

"Yea, I'm good. I don't know what came over me."

"I know what it was. It's called anger," Liam said sarcastically with a smirk on his face, wrapping his arms around her waist.

"Shut up, asshole," she spat back, trying to conceal her smile as she laid her head back on his shoulder.

"Aye, come on, let's go get the girls, then go see the boys. Oh yea, strap up just in case some shit pop off when we go get the girls," Yaseer stated as he walked off to his car, more than ready to see his girls, as well as go meet and spend time with his newborn sons.

Yaseer hopped in his all-black Charger and turned up Dej Loaf's song *Try Me*. That had become his anthem because that's what niggas had been trying to do to him lately, and just like she said, let a nigga try him and he was going to get their whole muhfuckin' family.

Yaseer sped off to meet up with the cats that knew where his girls were being held. Twenty minutes later, he was pulling up to a house on North Tryon that they trapped out of sometimes, with his crew pulling up right behind him. He honked the horn to signal for the boys to come on so that they could go get Chaunte and Madison. No sooner than he beeped the horn, Cake and Julez were coming down the porch stairs ready to put in work. They were like the grim reaper split in two when it came to bodying niggas. So Yaseer felt good having them on his team. Yaseer popped the locks as Cake reached the passenger side of his car.

"What up, Cake," Yaseer said, giving him a pound once Cake got settled in the car with his seatbelt secured.

"Ain't none," Cake responded. Yaseer looked in his rearview mirror to make sure Julez was in the car with Kai'yan, turned up his music, and then sped off. His destination was Atlanta, GA.

***

"Have you heard from Kai or Yaseer yet?" Paris questioned as she woke up from her sleep.

"Not yet," Brooklyn replied, looking down at Yaseer Junior in her arms, whom they decided to nickname YJ. He looked so much like Yaseer it was borderline scary. She was hoping he would open his eyes up so she could see if he had the same color in them as Liam and their late Grandfather Joe.

"Hey, auntie's man. Hey there, angel," Brooklyn cooed as she rubbed his tiny hand. She had fallen head over heels for her newborn nephew. She looked over at Paris, who was sitting up in her hospital bed breastfeeding Jaseer. He too looked like Yaseer, but you could see a little more of Paris in him than his little brother.

"Sssoooo what made you switch from naming him Naseer to Yaseer Junior?" Brooklyn questioned, making small talk, hoping that one of the boys or London would call her soon so that they would know that everything was alright. No sooner than the thought crossed her mind, her phone was going off before Paris could respond to her question.

"Hey, bae," Brooklyn answered in a sing-song voice.

"What up, shawty?" Kai'yan replied.

"Nothing much, just holding my handsome nephew," Brooklyn responded as she looked down at the baby.

"Cool, we will be up there sometime late tonight. We heading out now to get the girls."

"OMG. Yaaaaassss, finally," Brooklyn squealed excited-ly. She was more than ready to see her nieces. "Wait, you said y'all heading out? Heading out where?" Brooklyn questioned.

"To the A."

"Atlanta? The hell this bitch had my nieces all the way up there?"

"Yea, but don't worry, everything gucci. A'ight, ma, I'm fuck with you later and don't yo ass go into labor while we gone either," Kai'yan spat.

"As if I could stop the inevitable," Brooklyn said in a joking manner. Kai'yan couldn't help but laugh at her smart remark.

"Yea, a'ight, love ya, ma."

"Love you, too, hun, talk to you later and be safe," Brooklyn replied before disconnecting the call.

Chapter 3

"So I take it everything is going good so far?" Paris asked inquisitively.

"Yep, you know our boys and sis get down. They said they will be up here sometime late tonight."

"Ok, cool."

Paris and Brooklyn talked for a little while longer until Paris ended up falling asleep with Jaseer in her arms. Brooklyn stood up and walked over to the hospital's crib and put YJ down. Then she went and got Jaseer out of Paris' arms and did the same with him as she had done with YJ. After she had completed her task, she grabbed a blanket and sheet out of the closet beside the couch, spread the sheet out over the couch, and then laid down. She pulled the blanket up until it was under her chin and nodded off.

"Aaarrgghh," Brooklyn yelled, being woke up out of her sleep by a pain in her lower abdomen, three hours later. She halfway sat up, holding her stomach.

"Aarrgghhh," she screamed out again, waking Paris up out of her sleep.

"Brook, you good?" she questioned in a sleep filled voice.

"I-I don't know, P. I'm having real bad contractions."

"Oh shit," Paris said, now fully awake after hearing that. Then she grabbed her call button and called for the nurse.

"How can I help you?" the nurse questioned on the intercom in the room.

"Um, I think my sister-in-law is going into labor," Paris replied as Brooklyn yelled out once more in pain.

"Oh ok, we'll be right there," the nurse said already getting up to make her way to Paris' room.

***

"Alright, y'all take them locks off them thangs and get ready just in case shit go south," Yaseer spat on speaker phone to Kai'yan as they turned on the street where the house the girls were being held was located. Everyone already had their gear on, including their vests with their tools loaded and cocked, they were ready for whomever and whatever stood in the way of getting the girls. Yaseer's eyes scanned through the neighborhood, looking for the address he had been given. As he creeped through the neighborhood to his destination in his blacked out Charger, he spotted the faces of a few hustlas standing next to the house he was heading to. Yaseer parallel parked in front of the house where the girls were, more than ready to get his girls in his arms and get on through. He cut of the ignition to his car, grabbed his tools, and then hopped out of the car, ready for whatever, followed by his crew. They were silently hoping that someone would pop off so they could put something hot in their chest. Yaseer stopped his stride and looked next door at the dudes who were standing in front of the house hustling.

"Aye, you, what's ya name?" Yaseer asked the guy that was eyeballing them.

"Gutta, why?"

"Say, bruh, who live in this house?" Yaseer questioned, bypassing Gutta's *why* question.

"That's Ms. Jillian and my girl Erin's house. Why?"

"Come 'ere," Yaseer requested, yet again bypassing Gutta's *why* question.

Gutta pulled his True Religion jeans up and walked over to where Yaseer and The Torture Crew stood, looking on.

"Sup?" Gutta said, muggin' Yaseer.

"Ain't shit up, walk up here with us and knock on the door. Oh, and don't try no funny shit, or I will leave yo' last thoughts on the ground," Yaseer spat, then continued making his way down the walkway, up the stairs, and to the porch with their guest in tow. Yaseer leaned on the side of the door frame with his piece aimed at Gutta's waist as Gutta opened the screen door, then knocked on the door.

"Who is it?" a soft female's voice called out.

"Gutta."

Yaseer stood to his full height when he heard the locks being unlocked, ready for whatever drama awaited him on the other side of the door. As soon as Erin began opening the door, Yaseer pushed Gutta inside followed by himself, Zyon, Liam, London, Cake, Julez, and Kai'yan. Kai'yan shut the door behind him, since he was the last to enter. Yaseer paid no mind to the girl that had fallen on the floor upon his forced entry, being that as soon as he walked in, he spotted his girls sitting in front of the TV with toys and snacks in front of them, watching Veggie Tales. He almost broke out in a sprint to them once he laid eyes on them. Tears welled up in his eyes once he reached them and scooped them up in his arms. Yaseer stood there holding his seeds as close as he could to him, while placing kisses on their tiny faces. At that moment nothing could have made him a happier man.

"Aye, Seer!" Liam called out. For a moment, Yaseer had forgotten where he was until he heard Liam calling his name.

"Yea," Yaseer responded with a baritone voice full of emotion.

"Um, I think you need to come see this," Liam replied.

Yaseer's eyebrows knitted together as he thought about what could possibly be wrong that it needed his immediate attention. Yaseer walked over to where his crew was standing to see what had captured their attention. He stopped once he got to Liam and followed Liam's gaze. What he saw made him beyond befuddled.

"London, come get the girls," he ordered, not taking his eyes off what had his and all of his crew's attention.

London walked over to Yaseer, took the girls out of his arms, and balanced one on each of her hips. For babies that were only pushing two years of age, they were certainly chunky and tall, which made them heavy. London was two seconds away from putting them down but didn't want nothing to happen, being that they were in the house of the person that had kidnapped the girls. So instead, she walked over to Liam and passed him Chaunte. With one, it wasn't so bad.

Once the twins were secured, they all just stood in silence, looking on in confusion. Someone really had some explaining to do, and the only people that Yaseer knew could shed light on this was his parents. Yaseer looked into the face of a girl, who, if he just saw her walking down the street, he would have thought it was Brooklyn. The only differences were that she was thicker in the thigh and hip area, and instead of wearing her hair long like Brooklyn, she opted for a long layered bob with a swoop in the front. Yaseer had to get his thoughts together because this shit was really getting bananas. He wondered just how strong his dad's genes were because it seemed like the men in their family produced nothing but twins. Before today, he would not have thought that so many twins could be born to one family.

"You're Erin?" Yaseer questioned, needing to make sure that was her name.

"Yes," Erin responded in a fearful tone.

"And Jillian is your mother?"

"Yes, but no one hardly calls her that anymore. Since I can remember, she went by Jaminah, which is actually her middle name. Jillian is her first name," Erin answered.

"Has she ever went by the name Adela?"

"Not to my knowledge, that would be a beyond crazy if she did, being that that was my grandmother's name who passed away a little over six months ago," Erin responded.

"What do you know about these babies you have obviously been babysitting?" Yasser questioned with malice laced through each word. Possible sibling or not, he was ready to burst her melon open just thinking about it, but just by looking at her and how well she had taken care of his daughters, it was clear she had no intention of harming the girls.

"She just told me that they were one her friends' daughters and needed me to watch them while she went out of town."

"I see, and you have two brothers, correct?" Yaseer questioned, already knowing the answer to the question.

"Yes, I had two brothers, but Ezra was killed in a robbery almost a year ago?" she replied with tears beginning to blind her eye sight. "Wait, how do you know my brothers?" Erin questioned with her fear turning into confusion.

Yaseer felt bad for her, but at the same time wanted to laugh at the thought that she actually believed her brother died in a robbery. *Boy, her mother could sure make up a fine Mother Goose tale,* Yaseer thought to himself.

"I will answer anything you want to know once I have determined you ain't know shit 'bout what's been going on this past year. Where is your other brother?"

"He went out of town with my mom to visit our dad."

"And your dad, what is his name?" Yaseer asked to see what name she would say before he busted her world wide open.

"Eric Davis."

"Shit," Yaseer mumbled under his breath to himself as he ran his massive hands over his fresh Caesar cut and down his face.

None of this was making since to him. How could he have siblings that neither his father nor mother ever mentioned to him? Yaseer refused to believe that his mother didn't know, and what made Brooklyn more special that she had the opportunity to grow up with them, unlike the others? Yaseer didn't know the answers but he was determined to find out because his parents' actions, more so his dad's actions, had become his consequences and he wasn't having that.

"Sweetheart, do you have any idea who I am or why I am even here, standing in your living room, ready to shoot anything that even moves the wrong way, like this coward over here in the corner who just let some random niggas burst up in my sister's house, and he didn't even try to put up a fight, even if his life was on the line?" Yaseer questioned as he pulled his weapon equipped with a silencer. "The only reason he still breathing at this present moment is because my seeds are in here and I'on wanna do that in front of them. They don't need to see that. They have been through enough already with yo crazy momma kidnapping them. Look, I'm sure you have plenty of questions, as do I, so go put on some longer pants and let's go," Yaseer demanded in a low tone, not knowing what to think.

Erin looked back and forth between Yaseer and his daughters.

Chapter 4

"Kidnapped? Wait, my mom did what? Wait, and we're what?" Erin shot off question after question after everything that Yaseer said finally hit her.

"I will explain everything on the way. Now could you please go put on some longer pants so we can go? The next time I ask, I promise it won't be as nice," Yaseer replied, getting more and more agitated by the moment.

"Go? Go where? I'm not going anywhere with you," Erin spat back as she finally stood up from her seated position on the floor.

Yasser looked at her with every bit of anger filling his handsome face. He was trying his hardest not to flip out on her but she was really pushing it. He had no time to stand there and argue, and there was no way in hell he was leaving her there. He figured they both had questions and needed answers.

"You know what? Never mind, you ain't even got to put on no longer pants. You 'bout to get in the car anyway. Now let's go," Yaseer spat with his tool aimed at her head, hoping that would get her moving. He knew he was going overboard, but she was being stubborn as hell at the wrong damn time.

Erin looked at Yaseer as if he had literally just lost his last brain cell. Her fear had long ago left and had been replaced with anger towards the man who was standing in her house with a gun to her head, accusing her mother of heinous crimes such as kidnapping. She looked over at Gutta, wondering why he was just sitting there like a bitch when this man had a gun to her head. She turned her dark chocolate orbs back to Yaseer, then back to Gutta, looking back and forth between the two before she shook her head with a chuckle.

"You know what, Gutta? Fuck you! You really gon' sit there while this nigga holdin' his piece to my head and ain't do shit? Hell, I got a better chance trusting them with my fuckin' life than you, 'cause yo pussy ass just sittin' there lookin' like boo-boo the fool. Matter fact, can I see yo tool right quick so I can blow the stupidity out of his head, please?" Erin turned and asked Yaseer.

Yaseer had to keep his laughter in. Yeah, she was definitely related with that hot ass temper and slick mouth. "Nah, shorty. You can't do that with my seeds in the room. Plus, yo little ass might turn around and try to shoot my black ass. Now come on, y'all, I gotta get back to wifey and my new seeds," Yaseer stated as he began walking to the door with his crew, girls, and new-found sister in tow.

"I ain't want yo ass anyway, hoe. I just liked what that mouth could do. Yo mom's pussy was sweeter than that shit between yo legs," Gutta spat, pissed that Erin would even think about pointing anything hot his way. Everyone paused their stride. It grated Yaseer's nerves to even be in the presence of a bitch ass nigga. He looked at Erin, back to Gutta, then back to Erin.

"Aye y'all, keep on going to the car with girls, we coming," Yaseer ordered. He looked back at Erin.

"You know what? Here. He talk too much," Yaseer spat as he passed Erin his .9mm, equipped with a silencer. As soon as she went to take the gun from Yaseer, he pulled it back, looking in her eyes.

"Now you try some dumb shit and I will blow yo shit to pieces. Don't play with me," Yaseer said as serious as a heart attack, making sure he kept eye contact with her to let her know he meant business.

Erin looked down at Yaseer's hand, and sure enough, he had another piece in his other hand, business end pointed to the floor.

"Get em, girl," Yaseer said as he let her take the gun he was handing her, then leaned back on the black leather couch in the living room to watch the live action. He honestly doubted she would shoot Gutta, but then again, he thought that if she was of any true relation to them, then popping a nigga would be nothing to her.

"Now what's that hot shit you speaking?" Erin questioned Gutta as she put one in the chamber and began walking towards where he stood leaning up against the wall beside the kitchen.

"You heard what da fuck I said, bitch," Gutta spat back. Erin nodded her head up and down, taking in everything he was spitting her way. Yaseer had to chuckle to himself because she sort of reminded him of himself when she nodded her head up and down while Gutta was steady talking junk. Yaseer had a feeling lil buddy would regret everything he had said. Erin aimed the .9mm at Gutta's dick.

"Wait, wait, wait, bae, I was only fuckin' with you. You know I say shit to piss you off but ion' mean it. You know you my heart," Gutta began pleading, hoping to soften her up.

"You may not have meant that, but I for damn sure mean this," Erin spat as she shot two into Gutta's manhood. Gutta screamed out in agony as he grabbed his crotch area and fell to the ground with blood seeping in between his massive hands. Yaseer scrunched up his face and grabbed his own crotch. He did not even want to think about anything hurting his dick. *"Damn, women are crazy as fuck,"* Yaseer thought to himself.

"Bitch," Gutta gritted out between his teeth as he rolled from side to side in pain, balled up in the fetal position.

"This nigga still talkin' shit after being shot in the dick. This nigga dumb as fuck," Yaseer thought to himself as he continued to watch the action.

"Oh you 'on't even know! I'm a bitch ah'ite. I been one of them, but you forgot to add the crazy part," Erin responded as she let off one final shot to his head, putting him out of his miserable existence.

"Now we can go," Erin spat as she headed in Yaseer's direction, not knowing what to think. Gutta was her first body, but for some reason, she didn't feel any kind of remorse. In a way she felt justified because of the things he had claimed he had done. In other words, he had hurt her feelings because she actually cared for him. *"Good thing I only let 'em eat da cookie,"* Erin thought to herself as she handed Yaseer his gun, then walked outside to the car, with Yasser in tow.

Yaseer walked over to where Kai'yan stood beside his car waiting on him.

"Aye, I need you, Cake, and Julez to hire a maid to cook and clean her house," Yaseer said to Kai'yan in a low voice, letting them know that he needed them to make any evidence of them being there disappear. He would get rid of his gun later, since they couldn't get rid of the body like they normally did. They all nodded their heads in understanding. Yaseer was about to go get in his car when he heard a scream and someone yelling *no* repeatedly. Yaseer had his tool ready to spit fire until he realized it was London screaming from inside the car. Yaseer rushed to Liam's car. Liam was already jumping out the car screaming before Yaseer could even reach the car.

"She gone, Yas. She gone, man," Liam screamed out in tears as he slid down the side of his all-black 2014 Chrysler 300.

"Who? Who gone, Lee?" Yaseer questioned with panic laced through his voice, knowing it had to be somebody close for Liam to be on the ground crying, which meant it was either Paris or Brooklyn. God knows it would kill him to lose either one.

Yaseer's eyes wandered over to Zyon, who was sitting on the hood of the car with a stone face that had tears falling freely. Zyon never much dealt with pain like anyone else would. He pretty much dealt with it behind closed doors. He had been like that since their parents had been sentenced. Yaseer's eyes wandered back to Liam, waiting on a response.

"Liam, what the fuck goin' on? Somebody betta tell me something real quick before I spaz the fuck out," Yaseer spat.

"Brook, man, she gone, bruh, she gone, man," Liam cried out heartbrokenly from the sudden grief.

"Fuck you mean she gone, gone where? Where the fuck she at, Lee? Don't play with me," Yaseer yelled frantically, trying his hardest not to think the worst.

"She dead, man. She gone. My sister gone, man," Liam screamed out with pain laced in every word he spat.

"Naw, man, you not 'bout to tell me she gone. You must've gotten the wrong information. Come on so we can get on the road to go see our sister and so I can prove to you she ain't dead. Watch, we gone get back and Brook gon' be right there, worried and talking shit about not keeping her informed on what went on with her nieces."

"Seer, what part of gone don't you understand?" Liam yelled as he stood to his feet, getting in Yaseer's face.

"London just talked to Paris. She had been trying to call us but said no one was answering. She left us voicemails, crying, telling us to call, saying it was an emergency. Brook-Brook," Liam sobbed out. "Man, she woke up in pain and bleeding. The doctors had to do emergency surgery, talking 'bout the placenta had detached or some shit so they needed to do an emergency C-section. Paris said something about Brooklyn had a blood clot that went to her- her heart and the doctors did everything they could but couldn't save her and the baby at the same time. She gone, man, she gone," Liam spat as his tears flowed even harder.

"No, man. No! You not 'bout to stand here and tell me my fucking sister is dead! You not 'bout to stand in my face and tell me that shit!" Yaseer yelled in Liam's face as his eyes teared up.

Hearing the commotion caused Kai'yan, Cake, and Julez to run back outside with their guns in their hands, ready for whatever. They looked left to right trying to figure out what was going on and who they needed to lay on their asses. Yaseer looked at Kai'yan, then it hit him dead in his chest that he was going to have to be the one to tell Yan. He honestly didn't think he could do it. He just couldn't bring himself to even think about, let alone tell anyone, that his baby sister was dead.

Chapter 5

"What's going on, Seer? What's all the commotion about? Yaseer, man, what's going on? What you and Liam crying for?" Yaseer couldn't even get the words out without literally getting sick to his stomach. "Liam?" Kai'yan questioned, looking in his direction since Yaseer wouldn't answer him. Liam didn't have the heart to tell him either, but someone had to, and from the looks of it, Yaseer was not the one who was going to be able to do the task.

"Broo- Brook gone, man," Liam choked out before he felt like his throat was being constricted and his heart ripped out of his chest. Once again, his tears began to run like water falls.

"She... She what?" Kai'yan muttered out, hoping he was hearing things.

"She's dead, Yan," London answered as she stepped out of the car with a tear stained face.

"Naw, man, naw. No!" Kai'yan screamed out in pain. "She can't be, man, we having a baby. Naw, man, she can't be dead," Yan spat as he walked back and forth, not believing his ears. "Not my girl, man. No, no, no, not my baby," Kai'yan mumbled more to himself than anyone. With the mention of the word baby passing through his lips, the thought of rather he and Brooklyn's baby made it or not beamed in his head like a light bulb.

"My baby, my baby, is it ok?" Kai'yan asked, praying their baby was okay.

"Yes, she is fine. I think we need to get on the road so that you can get to her and so we can check on Paris. She is dealing with this all alone. Come on, let's go. I will explain the details on the way," London answered in a calm voice before turning to speak to Cake and Julez. "Listen, y'all handle the details concerning Erin's house, then hop on the road. We will leave one of the cars here, but we have to go immediately," London told them in a quiet voice before going to the driver side of Liam's car, knowing that he wasn't going to be able to drive in the emotional state that he was in. Before she got inside, she looked over the hood to where Erin stood looking on, trying to figure out what was going on and who was Brooklyn. London caught a frog in her throat as she looked at her. She looked so much like Brooklyn it was borderline scary. Minus the few differences, Erin and Brooklyn were definitely identical twins.

"Aye, baby girl, you got L's, or nah?" London questioned once she got her emotions in check.

"Yea, I got a license," Erin replied.

"A'ight, get Yaseer's keys, get in the driver's seat, and follow me. Yaseer, Liam, and Kai'yan, let's go. I don't care who riding with who but we need to get on the road now. Oh, and Kai'yan, leave your keys for Cake and Julez so they can get back," London ordered as she got in the driver's seat and cranked the car up.

For a moment, the crew forgot their emotions and looked on as London took charge. Hurting and all, Yaseer couldn't help but to feel some sense of pride, seeing the true boss that London had grown into within the past year. As ordered, the crew followed London's demands, knowing that now was not the time to argue.

Yaseer got on the passenger side of his car and handed his keys to Erin as she adjusted his seat. He could hardly bring himself to look at her, being that she and Brooklyn looked just alike. Erin took the keys out of his hand, put the car in gear, and began following behind London as she led the way. She went to turn the music that was playing softly up a little and noticed the time on the clock. It was damn near 4:30 in the morning. She could not even believe she was up at this time of morning. She was normally sleep by nine o'clock, ten at the latest. She shook her head. This was not how she imagined her night turning out, but it was what it was.

***

Three hours and some change later, they were pulling into Presbyterian Hospital. No one was looking forward to getting out of the car. It was like a ton of bricks on their bodies, weighing them down. London was the first to get out of the car. She shut the car door and just leaned on it, trying to gather her thoughts and put her emotions in check because somebody was going to have to keep it together for Yaseer, Liam, Zyon, and Kai'yan. Otherwise, Charlotte's crime and missing rate would skyrocket because of their emotions.

The crew piled out of the cars one by one, with Yaseer being the last to get out. He was taking Brooklyn's death harder than anyone. As a big brother, he felt the need to always protect his baby sister. He would kill someone in the blink of an eye just to keep her protected, but what was he to do when it was her own body that had betrayed her. Just thinking about it made Yaseer want to go on a killing spree. He needed to kill something to make it at least feel like he was avenging his sister's death. But he was no fool, because, at the end of the day, no matter how many people he killed, Brooklyn would still be dead, his grief would still be there, and it would've all been for nothing because no matter what he did, she would never be in the land of the living again.

Yaseer wiped the tears that had once again started falling with the back of his hand and tried his hardest to at least get some of his emotions in check.

"Come on, bro-in-law, you got this." London touched his shoulder as she looked him in the face with tears sitting on the brim of her almond shaped eyes. "You know Brooklyn would go ham if she saw you crying. You know she always use to tell us if she went out first to make sure we threw her one big ass party to celebrate her life, not mourn it. I could see her cussing you out right now for crying over her. Now there is a beautiful baby girl in there, who happens to be your niece, who just lost a mommy that she will never know, and there is also two handsome young men in there, who have yet to meet their father, as well as your grieving fiancé."

Yaseer nodded his head up and down. London always had a way of making the worst situations seem like the best situations. Just knowing there was a little girl in there who would need their love and protection now more than ever helped him get his emotions even more in check. Yaseer looked inside of his car window at his little girls, who were fast asleep.

"Don't even worry about them. I got them. They have had a long day. I will take them home and put them to bed. You go ahead and deal with everything that is going on in there," London said as she used her index finger to point at the entrance of the hospital.

"Thanks, L. I truly appreciate this, I really do," Yaseer said in a low voice as he leaned down and gave London a hug, and then went inside the hospital, followed by everyone else, except London.

Chapter 6

"Hey, Erin," London called out. Erin turned around at the sound of her name being called.

"Yea," she responded back.

"Come 'ere," London replied.

Erin walked over to where London stood leaning up against Yaseer's car. "What's up?" Erin questioned, once she came face to face with London.

"Listen, you come with me. I know you may not understand everything, and I promise I will explain it to you, but right now, inside of there is not where you want or need to be at the moment. I will show you why once we get to my house. You still have Yaseer's keys?" London asked Erin, who just nodded her head up and down as she held the keys out to London for her to take. Both she and London climbed in Yaseer's 2014 blacked out Charger and pulled off. No less than an hour later, after stopping at the store and getting a few items for the twins, they were pulling up at London's humble abode, both tired from being up for twenty-four hours.

"You get one and I get the other," London suggested, referring to Chaunte and Madison, who were still fast asleep without a care in the world. As London had suggested, she retrieved Chaunte and Erin retrieved Madison, along with a few bags from the store.

"I'll come get the rest of the bags once we get them inside the house," London stated as she struggled to pull her keys out of her front pants pocket. Once she had her keys, she opened her door, and stood back to allow Erin to enter before her. Once Erin was all the way inside, she followed her and closed the door behind her, not even bothering to lock it, being that she was about to have to go right back out there to get the bags that were still left in the car. Erin's eyes bounced from left to right, looking around London's comfy house. She practically fell head over heels looking at London's seventy-eight-inch curved TV, along with her entertainment center, fireplace, black leather sectional, and end and coffee tables. The brown bricked wall behind London's entertainment center set everything else off in the living room and gave it that homey affect.

"You take her to the spare room. Follow me," London said, breaking Erin's ogling. London walked past her, leading the way to the spacious room. London walked over to the California King, pulled the black covers back, and laid Chaunte on the bed. Then she stepped aside to let Erin do the same thing. Once Erin finished tucking the twins in, she and London walked out of the room, leaving the room door cracked just in case one of the twins woke up. They walked down the short hallway that led back into her living room and sat down on her plush sofa.

"Ok, so let me make this long story short for you. Then you can ask away and I will answer your questions the best way that I can. Cool?"

"Yeah, that's cool," Erin responded.

"Alright, I'm not even sure exactly where to begin. The babies that were under your care are Yaseer's daughters. Your mother kidnapped them as revenge for, as she says, 'Yaseer killing Ezra.' I'm not sure how much she has told you about your father, but Yaseer and Ezra had the same father. Technically, Yaseer and Ezra were cousins as well as brothers because your mom is Yaseer's mom's little cousin. No one knew this until Ezra told everyone before he died. Ezra did a lot of hurtful shit to everyone in our crew, just to hurt Yaseer. He raped Yaseer's fiancé, slept with Yaseer's baby's mother, and made sure Paris found out about

Yaseer's secret children, which happens to be the babies you were watching. He plotted Yaseer's demise, all the while smiling in his face, pretending to be his best friend, and helping to find the person who was behind the pain and hurt that had come upon the crew, when all along it was him causing the pain. Last but not least, he almost killed Yaseer, Liam, and Zyon's baby sister, Brooklyn, which is who just passed away while doctors were doing a C-section on her to deliver her and Kai'yan's baby. Now here is where a little confusion comes in, and why everyone was ogling you at your house."

London grabbed her phone off of the table, went to her Facebook account, and pulled up Brooklyn's page so that she could show Erin her and Brooklyn's freaky resemblance. "This is why I advised you not to go into the hospital. It would be too much on everybody right now. Hell, I'm surprised I am even able to be in the same vicinity as you right now," London spat as she passed Erin her phone after finding a good picture of Brooklyn.

Erin stared at the picture in shock, then a wave of sadness hit her. The girl she was staring at could pass for her any day and time. It was clear that they were definitely identical twins. Her life had been a lie. Her mother never told her she had other siblings. She lied about who the babies were, about the way Ezra had died, and why he died. From what her mother had told her, her dad was locked up, and that's why he never came to see her. She had seen pictures of him and talked to him on the phone, but who's to say that her mother wasn't lying about who her real father was.

"Wooh, this is a lot to take in. Um, I- I have a question. My- my mom always told me that my dad was in prison and that is why he was not around while I was growing up. I have seen pictures of him, but after all this, who's to say she wasn't lying about that too. Do- do you happen to have any pictures of him?" Erin questioned, hoping that at least her mom had told the truth about who her biological father was.

"I don't have one, but I am almost certain that Brooklyn has a picture of him on her page. Let me see," London responded, holding out her hand for her phone. Erin handed London her phone and watched as London went through Brooklyn's photos, only to stop on a picture of a man and tap on it to enlarge the photo for her to see. "Is this him?" London questioned, showing Erin the photo, knowing good and well that she was Eric's daughter.

Chapter 7

"Yep, that's him. I actually have that picture at home in my photo album. He had some pictures sent to me for me to have of him. Is he really locked up?"

London nodded her head up and down before responding. "Yes, he is. Some bullshit went down, and he and his wife both got knocked. Actually, Mrs. Davis will be getting out soon," London replied.

"Damn. So basically Yaseer, Liam, Zyon, Ezra, Juice, Brooklyn, and myself are all siblings with the exception of myself, Brooklyn, Juice, and Ezra being their cousins as well."

"Yup," London answered as she leaned her head back on her couch and closed her eyes. So much had happened in the past year and a half it was a wonder any of them were still sane.

"Well, I'm beat, so I'm about to go K.O. and we will discuss this more in the morning. Come on, I will show you where you will be sleeping tonight," London spat as she leaned forward, got up off the couch, and began walking to the other side of her house, through the kitchen area. She walked to an area that led to another hallway where another bedroom was located and opened the door.

"You can sleep in here tonight. The closet in the bathroom and it has some clean towels, wash cloths, sheets, and blankets. It's fully stocked. Tomorrow we will go to the mall and get you a few things, since you don't have any clothes with you," London said as she turned around to exit.

"Hey, London, why... do you know why Yaseer brought me back. Like he's- he's not going to kill me, is he?" Erin stammered out.

London couldn't help but laugh. She and Brooklyn may have looked alike but they were as opposite as night and day. Brooklyn would have been like, "Tell that nigga he try and kill me and I will take his soul along with mine."

"Naw, sweetie, if he was going to kill you, he would have did that the moment he entered yo crib. I'm sure he has questions, as I'm pretty sure everyone else does. Now it's been a long day, get some rest, love," London replied as she walked out of the room toward her room.

By the time she had reached her room, she had decided instead of going right to bed, she wanted to take a shower before she laid down. She needed to ease her mind and a shower would do just that. She shut her room door and stripped down out of her clothes until she was nude. She picked up her discarded clothes, put them in the laundry basket, and headed to the shower. London shut the bathroom door upon her entrance. She opened the shower door, turned the water on, and adjusted the temperature to as hot as she could stand it. Then she stepped in with her back towards the hot steamy water. She took a few steps back, inhaled a deep breath, then exhaled as she tilted her head back to let the hot water run over hair and face. Using her hands, she pushed the water out of her face. She stood there for a minute just basking in the warmth of the water as it cascaded down her back before picking up her dove soap and her rag. She lathered her rag up, then proceeded to wash all of the past twenty-four hours off of her body. After she was sure that soap had reached every part of her skin, she rinsed off. After the traces of soap were completely unseen, she placed her rag over the shower bar that she had built inside of her shower.

London turned around so that the front of her body was facing the water, then sat down on the shower floor just to enjoy the water and let it relax her. London sat there with water running over body, thinking of everything that had transpired in the last twenty-four hours. She could not believe that Brooklyn was gone. Not in a million years did she think Brooklyn would be gone this soon. But as fate would have it, she was indeed gone. She had been so strong for everyone else that she, herself, didn't take a minute to grieve over her best friend, who had become more like a sister to her over the years. For the first time since she heard the news, she let the wave of emotions hit her heart and let the pain of it all exit from her eyes. Heartbroken did not even begin to explain how she felt. Neither she nor Paris kept a lot of friends growing up, so when they met Brooklyn and became friends with her, they had finally gotten what they had always longed for, a true friend.

London put her head in her hands and had one of the biggest cries that she had had in a very long time. She was crying so hard she didn't even hear the footsteps that were coming towards the shower door, nor did she hear the shower door open. London damn near jumped out of her skin when she felt someone touch her. Her eyes locked in with the man that had caught her at her most vulnerable moment as she had done to him. No words were needed as he outstretched his hand to help her stand, and pulled her into his embrace. London laid her head on Liam's chest and broke down crying even harder.

Liam held London tighter as he broke down crying with her as well. He needed her strength just about as much as she needed his. He wondered if this was God's way of punishing them for killing their brother. But he reasoned that it was just her time and that maybe God needed her more than they did. No matter the reasoning, the pain he felt was like none other and at that moment, he needed London more than ever. Yes, he needed her strength, but he needed to feel her love even more. Point blank period, he needed her, all of her. He knew it was selfish because she was hurting just as he was, but at that moment, he felt like he deserved to be selfish and downright greedy, if it took his pain away for even a second.

Liam pulled back a little and took his index finger and tilted her head back so that he could see her beautiful face. Through puffy eyes, they both stared each other down, both of their faces revealing every emotion in their souls. Liam took his right hand and held the side of London's face, then began using the pad of his thumb to rub back and forth across her high cheekbone. Liam continued to gaze into her beautiful chocolate orbs before leaning forward and placing a sweet short kiss on her luscious lips. After slightly pulling back, he repeated the process. This time, instead of pulling back, he deepened the kiss and pulled her body closer to his. With London in his embrace, Liam began easing London backwards until her back hit the warm tiled wall. Liam glided his hands over London's silky wet curves until his massive hands landed on the back of her thighs. Grasping tightly, Liam picked her up and pushed her body into the wall.

London wrapped her legs around his trim waist, wrapped her arms tighter around his neck, and pulled him closer to her. London gasped and tilted her head back as she felt Liam's manhood begin to enter the portal of her very essence.

Liam continued to push into London until he was at the hilt. His breath caught at the feeling. He swore to himself that there was no better feeling in the world than being inside of the woman that he loved. No matter how bad his day had been, just being inside of her made him feel like all of his sorrows in life had been snatched away. He never wanted to lose that feeling.

London's fingernails dug into Liam's shoulder at the feeling of him moving in and out of her body. She thought she would die right there in his arms once she started feeling the tip of his steel rubbing against her G-spot. London began to move her hips, putting out just as much action as she was receiving.

Liam's mouth found its way to the side of her neck where he began to place soft subtle kisses in between sucking on it, making sure to leave his mark. Liam slowed his pace just a tad to enjoy the feeling of London being wrapped around his member like a glove.

London placed her hand on the back of Liam's head as to keep his head stationed on the side of her neck. Between the feeling of his tongue on her neck and his piece pumping in and out of her, London thought she would literally explode into a billion pieces. It was at that moment she knew without a doubt in her mind that he was the man that she would follow to the ends of the earth and back. Not because of how he was making her body feel, but because in their moment of pain, he found a way to take the pain that they were both feeling away, even if it was only for a brief moment. Just that brief moment without pain gave her the extra strength she needed to make it through the next day. For the first time since they had begun making love, she gave him her all as he gave her his. Moments later, they both released their essence upon one another.

Liam rested his forehead on London's as he attempted to catch his breath before he slowly began easing out of her, and releasing her legs so that she could put her feet on the shower floor. Grabbing her hands, Liam pulled her into the warm water, grabbed the dove shower wash, lathered her rag up, and began washing her body from head to toe before he lathered his own rag and washed himself up as well. Once they were both rinsed off, Liam turned the water off, opened the shower door, grabbed one of the fluffy black towels that hung on the towel rack beside the shower, opened it up, and wrapped it around London. Then he stepped back so that he could let her out first before he repeated the process for himself. In silence, they both walked into the bedroom where they finished drying off, got into bed, and drifted off into a deep sleep.

Chapter 8

London awoke the next morning to the sun beaming in her eyes. She lifted her head off of Liam's chest, who was still fast asleep with his arm wrapped around her waist. She gently removed his hand and slid out of the bed. After going to the bathroom to empty her bladder, she slipped on a black sports bra, some black sweats and socks. She looked back over her shoulder at Liam, smiled, and shook her head. Making sure not to make too much noise, she quietly opened the door and slipped out before closing the door. She walked down to the spare room she had placed the twins into to check on them. They were still knocked out. Then she made a beeline straight to the refrigerator and grabbed a cran-grape Ocean Spray juice and then headed over to the room that she had stationed Erin in last night.

London knocked lightly before gently opening the door, just in case Erin was still asleep. London peeped her head in and caught Erin trying to hurriedly wipe the tears that had clearly been falling down her beautiful face. London walked in and closed the door behind her. She walked over to Erin, sat down beside her, and pulled her into her arms so that Erin could let it all out. She rubbed her back as Erin's tears once again started to flow heavily down her face. London continued to hold her until she heard Erin began to calm down. She pulled back a little so that she could do a little investigation to find out what was the cause of the water-work show that had just happened.

"Now come on, tell me the reason for these tears, hun."

For a moment, Erin hesitated. London was practically a complete stranger to her so pouring her heart out to her was something she was sort of iffy about. But after thinking about it some more, she realized she had no one else to talk to or that would understand her. She cast her eyes downward before taking a deep breath and looking up at London.

"For the first time in my life, I am truly alone. My family's gone. I don't have friends, and I don't fit in nor do I belong here. I'm just here, and I don't even know why I'm here. What was the purpose of bringing me here? What am I going to do without my mom and brothers? They're all I know. Now they're gone. I want to blame that stupid man who made me even come, but then in a way, I know I can't blame him because what my mom and brothers did was wrong. They knew it would be consequences, and I can't blame that man for killing them. I probably would have done the same thing, especially after what they did, but- but it still hurts like hell. I know y'all just lost someone, but where you all lost one, I have lost three," Erin concluded before looking off to the side, thinking of how her calm world had literally just gotten turned upside down.

London looked down at her hands to try and gather the correct words to say to Erin before she spoke her mind. She didn't want to come off as a bitch, but the last part sort of irked her for some reason.

"Listen, sweetie, I'm 'bout to spit some hot shit to you real quick. First off, that man that you're speaking of is your brother and his name is Yaseer. Second, you are not alone. I know you do not know us that well, but in due time you will. You have three brothers that are alive and kicking and that I am sure would go to bat for you. And you have myself and Paris, who happens to be your future sister-in-law, who would shoot a fly off the map to protect you if need be. Third of all, I know you may think that we only lost one person, but I have lost two, which is Brooklyn and, believe it or not, Ezra. I truly loved him like he was my own blood. Yaseer, Zyon, and Liam have lost four people. They lost their parents to the prison scene. They just lost their baby sister. Then, on top of that, they lost a friend who has been around them their whole childhood, only to find out right before he died that he was not only their friend, but also their brother slash cousin. So they have lost just as much as you, if not more. Baby girl, we all lose and have lost people, but it is up to you if you want to lose yourself in the ones that were lost in this battle called life. It's up to you. Just know that you are not alone. You have people here for you. And if I were you, I would start getting to know the ones that share the same blood as me. Now whichever one you choose to begin with, that is up to you, but please, please don't ever think that you are alone because you're not," London said in a soft voice as she took her hand and rubbed the top of Erin's hand before standing up to leave the room.

London turned around to exit the room and damn near jumped out of her skin when she saw Liam standing in the doorway with his arms crossed across his bare chest.

"Liam," London called as she cleared her throat before finishing her statement. "I didn't...We didn't hear you come in."

"I went searching for you and heard you talking to someone. I was curious, so I came to see who you was talking to this early in the morning. I was hoping you hadn't nutted up on a nigga and was talking to yo'self and shit," Liam replied with a smirk on his handsome face.

"Shut up," London replied, trying hard not to laugh at Liam's joke, but failing miserably. "Come on so we can go fix breakfast before the girls wake up," London said as she began walking towards the door, past Liam.

"You go head, L, lemme holla at my newfound little sis for a min," Liam said as London made it out the door.

"Okay, I will go ahead and get everything started. Take your time," London responded as she rubbed his arm and stood on her tippy toes to give him a quick peck on the lips before making her way to the kitchen.

Liam looked over and watched London's ass as she walked away. He shook his head. Shawty had his head gone. Liam stepped into the room, shut the door, and walked over to where Erin sat on the bed looking down at her hands. Being around him, as well as Yaseer and Zyon, made her nervous. She didn't know why, but it did. Liam grabbed the chair that sat at the vanity mirror and sat the chair right in front of Erin before he sat down in the seat. For a minute, it seemed like time had stopped. He just sat and literally stared at the woman, whom he had just found out was the twin to his baby sister, who was now dead. It was kind of weird looking at her because she and Brooklyn resembled one another, but so far physical appearance was where their similarities seemed to end. After sitting in silence for a few moments, Liam finally decided to speak.

"You know she was on point, right?" Liam didn't even wait for her to respond. "You not alone. Yeah, this is real fucked up for us to meet a sister, who we didn't even know existed, around the same time that our sister, who we have known our whole lives, passes away and you and her happen to be identical twins. No, it won't be easy street because it is going to take time to get used to seeing the face of our baby sister every day, who is now deceased. It's like she's gone but she's not because we will see her every time we look at you, ya dig? But please do not think you're alone cause uggghhh ion know if L told you, but we gone be on yo ass like white on rice, especially Yaseer. When this year ends, you gon wish you could have a damn moment alone. So cheer up, kiddo," Liam spat with a slight smile on his face.

"Come on, let's go help L fo' she kick our ass," Liam said over his shoulder as he exited the room.

Liam walked into the kitchen, followed by Erin. London had just put a fresh batch of beat eggs in a pan and was putting sausages in the pan she had warming up beside it.

"What you need us to do, shawdy?" Liam questioned as he walked up behind her, put his arms around her, and nestled his chin in the crook of her neck.

"Umm, you can put the batter in the waffle iron for me."

"Okay, cool," Liam replied as he released her from his embrace and then smacked her on the ass before going to complete the task she had assigned to him.

"And, Erin, you can make the grits, if that's fine with you. Hold up, wait, can you cook? Ion' want you burning my shit up and ion want no soupy or pasty grits either. Ion' play 'bout my food na."

Erin couldn't help but chuckle at the alarm in London's voice. "Yes, I can cook. I been cooking full meals since I was ten years old. If my momma ain't do nothing else right, she did teach us how to cook right."

"Alright na, fuck up my food and we gon' have it out. You better ask Liam," London spat.

Liam looked at Erin and silently shook his head *no*. Erin tried to conceal her smile that was beginning to show itself. London saw Erin trying not to smile and swung her pretty little head back to look at Liam. When she turned, he was nodding his head up and down, agreeing with her. Erin could no longer hold her smile. She could already tell her brother was a mess. He seemed cool, and she liked that.

"Alright, Liam, lie to her if you want to. You know ion' play 'bout my food. Anywho, let's go ahead and get this food done and eat so we can get up to the hospital. I want to go see the babies, and check on Paris, as well as the boys, to see how they holding up. Liam and Erin both nodded their heads up and down and got to going about their tasks.

"Is it okay with you guys if I just stay here? I don't think everyone is comfortable with being around me just yet and vice versa. Plus, the girls are still asleep, no point in waking them up."

"You sure, boo? I mean, eventually everyone will have to get used to you being around."

"Yea, I know. I'm just not ready yet, and neither are they. Hell, actually, I'm just getting kind of comfortable being around you guys."

"Yea, I feel you on that, hun. Well, alright then."

Less than an hour later, the twins were up, the food was done and everyone's bellies were full. Now they were getting dressed and prepared to leave out to go meet up with the crew at the hospital. As soon as they stepped out of the door, Liam's ringtone went off. Liam pressed the answer button on his Bluetooth that went around his neck to accept the phone call. He already knew who it was when he heard the ringtone.

"What up, bruh-bruh?"

"Where y'all at?"

"We on the way, Seer. We'll be there in like twenty something minutes. We just now leaving the house," Liam spat into the receiver as he hopped in the driver's seat of his all-black Chrysler 200, followed by London. Once they were strapped down in their seat belts, Liam cranked the car up, turned on his music, pulled out of London's driveway, and began making his way to the hospital.

Chapter 9

"They on the way?" Paris questioned.

"Yeah," Yaseer answered as he made his way to the window.

He put one palm on the wall beside the window and just stood, looking out over downtown Charlotte, just thinking about his life and everything that had happened in the past year. He had done so much in the streets of Charlotte, NC for one reason and one reason only, and that was so that his family or himself would never have to want for nothing else again in their lives. Anything they wanted or needed, they could buy, they had love, and above all else, they had each other... They had family. Not once did he ever think that this was how things would turn out. He and his crew had gained more power than either of them could deal with. They could sway witnesses, and had cops, judges, FBI agents, the DA, and all in their pockets, hence the reason why after Paris had gotten out, no one in their crew had ever been arrested. But no matter how much power, money, love, or control they had, they couldn't control one thing, a natural death. There was no way any of them could control it, and as bad as Yaseer wanted to be mad at God and blame him for taking his baby sister, he couldn't. And as much as he wanted to blame himself, he couldn't do that either because she didn't die by the hands of one of their enemies. He wanted to blame his newborn niece, but he couldn't do that either because she was innocent. He could however blame Kai'yan for getting her pregnant, but then again, no, he couldn't, because it took two to tango.

For the first time, neither his gun nor torturing devices could help him exact revenge because they had no one to exact revenge on. The only thing that Yaseer could officially blame was life itself. The only thing he was mad at himself for was the fact that he was not there to at least get to say goodbye or see her beautiful smile one more time before she passed on. Yaseer was deep in thought when he felt a delicate hand on his shoulder. Startled only a little bit, he looked over his left shoulder to see Paris standing behind him with mixed emotions on her face, but there were two emotions he saw on her face above all others, and that was her love and concern for him, as well as another emotion... Grief.

Yaseer dropped the hand that he had been using to hold his weight as he leaned on the side of the window to look out and brought it around Paris' waist with his other hand following behind. He pulled her close to him and just embraced her before leaning his head down and placing his forehead on hers. For a moment, they just stood there in silence, holding one another.

"Thank you," Yaseer whispered in a soft voice.

"For what? I haven't done anything to be thankful for."

"For being here. For always just being here. With me. I appreciate all the times you have been there for me, but right now, at this moment when you have your own grief that you are trying to deal with, yet you're standing here in front of me tryna be strong for me." Yaseer paused and just stared at her as he took his right hand, lifted it to her beautiful face, and let his fingertips caress the side of it before continuing on with his statement. "And, and I appreciate that, so thank you," Yaseer said before guiding his fingertips to the tip of her chin and tilting her head back. His eyes traveled to her lips before he ducked his head down to her plump lips. Giving her a quick soft gentle kiss on her lips, he pulled back and just gazed at her as if it was his first time seeing her. Paris lifted her hand and wrapped it around his.

"Seer, ain't no need to thank me, that shit automatic. Just like I'm here for you, I know without a shadow of a doubt in my brain that you would be here for me without hesitation if something had happened to London. So save ya thank yous, love," Paris spat as she pulled him into a tight embrace and laid her head on his chest.

Yaseer pondered what she had just said, and for once, he had no comeback because what she had just said was one hundred percent true. If it had been London, he would have been there for her, no doubt, no matter if they were together or not, he would have still been there for her. Yaseer just held on to her as he let the feeling of her touch calm his broken soul. Yaseer rested the side of his face on top of her head. As soon as he had gathered his thoughts to say something back to Paris, he heard someone walk in. He lifted his head and damn near had a heart attack at who he saw standing behind Paris. His mind had to be playing tricks on him. He had to blink his eyes a couple of times to make sure that he wasn't seeing things due to the stress he had been having, but nope, his eyes were legit seeing the person standing behind them.

"Mom," Yaseer called out just above a whisper as his embrace on Paris loosened.

"Don't mom me, you better come on over here and give me some sugar."

"Oh shit, I mean shoot. My B, ma," Yaseer spat as he dropped his embrace around Paris, walked over to his mom, and gave her a hug and a kiss. He didn't know what to think or how to react. His mom was supposed to have another year left. So he was shocked to see her standing there.

"Ma, what are you doing here? When did you get out? I thought you had another year to do. Wait, how did you know where we were?" Yaseer shot off question after question before he finally paused to let his mom even get a word in, which was after she called his name multiple times for him to allow her to do so.

"First off, before I answer anything, would you move out of the way so that I may show my future daughter some love? And where is my grandbabies? I wanna see 'em."

"Hold up, we will get to all of that in a few minutes. When did you get released? And why didn't I know that you were getting out early?"

"Alright, I see you're still impatient as ever. Damn, I swear you act just like your father sometimes. I just got out three days ago. I didn't tell you that I was getting out early because I wanted it to be a surprise. I had planned to wait until your birthday next week, but soon as I heard about Brooklyn, I got on the next thing smoking. Where is Liam and Zyon?"

"Liam is on the way, oh shit, wait, ma, I got some to tell you. Ma, ugh. Ma, did whoever you speak with, wait, who did you speak to? Who knew you were coming?"

"I spoke to Zyon but he had no idea I was coming, or that I was out. However, as soon as he mentioned about my newborn grandbabies and Brooklyn, I was on my way."

"Did he happen to mention anything about a girl named Erin?" Yaseer questioned, praying to God he would not have to be the one to tell his mom about her. It seemed like he was always the one left to do the dirty job.

"No, he didn't mention her. Who is she?" Before Yaseer could answer his mom's question about who Erin was, there was a slight knock on the door before Liam walked in, followed by Zyon, Kai'yan, and London.

Chapter 10

Mrs. Davis turned around just as the crew piled up in the room. It took a few moments after heys, kisses, and hugs had been given out before she finally turned her attention over to Paris.

"Oh my goodness there's that beautiful face that just gave me some grandboys!" She said with excitement as she walked over to Paris who was now sitting up on the edge of her hospital bed, bent down and gave her a huge hug.

"How you feeling baby?" She questioned.

"I'm a little sore but other than that I must say I'm ok." Paris replied.

"Well hopefully that soreness will go away soon. I remember when I gave birth to those two knuckle heads over there. I didn't ever think I would heal." She said as she looked over at her handsome sons.

"Speaking of... I hate to bring this up at a moment such as this, but I have to. Ma did you know that Brooklyn had a twin sister?" Yaseer questioned.

"A twin sister?! I most certainly did not. Who told you that lie?" Mrs. Davis asked in an irate tone.

"Nobody had to tell us anything ma." Liam answered as he pulled his phone from his pocket scrolled over to the gallery and pulled up the picture he had downloaded of Erin earlier that day from her Facebook, then held his phone out for his mom to see. She walked slowly to the phone before finally getting close enough to glance at the picture.

"Who you boys think you foolin'? That's damn Brooklyn!"

"Ma, no it's not."

"I know what the damn chile I raised look like and I know she ain't got no damn twin. Yo daddy would have never kept that from me. Now why in the hell did you call me and tell me Brooklyn was dead! What kind of fuckery is this shit? Zyon, what on God's green earth could be so bad in life that you would speak death on your baby sister. Why would you do something so cruel?" Mrs. Davis spat as she dug daggers into Zyon's piercing eyes.

Before he could get any kind of smart remark out, Yaseer intervened and answered the question their mom had been waiting on an answer to.

"Ma, Zyon didn't speak anything on Brooklyn. She's really gone. However, the woman that you see in that photo in front of you is Erin. The girl I mentioned to you before everyone else got here. She is Brooklyn's identical twin," Yaseer said as he rubbed a hand down his handsome face, then crossed his arms across his chest as he waited on a response.

"Wait, wait. So your telling me that your dad has kept this from me all these years?" Mrs. Davis asked in a cool voice.

"I guess so because Erin is definitely Brooklyn's twin. We have actually been in her presence."

"Ima kill em" Yaseer heard his mom mumble. He couldn't help but lean his head to the side and study her expression before deciding to ask his next question.

"So Ma, you really 'bout to sit here and tell me, tell us, that you seriously had no clue? Brooklyn had an identical twin sister that you absolutely knew nothing about?"

"No, I, I... No, I didn't know she had a twin sister. Now if you all will excuse me, I need to excuse myself," Mrs. Davis replied in a stern voice as she made a quick exit to the door.

Before she could open it all the way, Yaseer spoke. "Don't go too far, ma. It's good to have you home again," Yaseer spat with a slight smirk on his face.

With a quick nod of her head, she swiftly made her exit. She couldn't stand in the same room with them at that moment. It fucked with her too much. Hearing and actually seeing that Brooklyn most definitely had an identical twin brought back too many painful memories. Memories that she would just love to leave in the past.

The crew stood looking at the door like they had just seen Casper the ghost himself leave the room. Yaseer was the first to break the silence.

"She's lying," he spat with his face twisted up like he had just tasted something that was bitter. Everyone's head snapped back in his direction like a rubber band.

"How you know she lying, Seer? You ain't no muhfuckin' lie detector. If ma said she ain't know nothin' 'bout Erin, then she ain't know nun. Who da hell are you to question her word? Fuck she got to lie to yo ass for?" Zyon popped off with venom laced throughout his words.

"Nigga, who the fuck you think you talking to? I will bust yo head to da muhfukin' white meat and won't think twice about the shit. Don't you ever question me again as long as you got breath in yo dumb ass body, and I mean that shit," Yaseer threw back at Zyon as he took a step towards Zyon, ready for whatever. It was not the day for Zyon to test his G. He loved his little brother to death but with the way he was feeling at that moment, he would beat Zyon unconscious without even realizing he had done so until it was too late. That's just how mad he was.

"Who da fuck you think you poppin' that hot shit to, Yaseer. I ain't scared of yo bitch ass, not one bit. Ain't not one piece of the blood that's flowing through my veins got hoe in it. Now, nigga, if you feeling froggy, then go on head and leap over that lily pad, Kermit. Oh yeah, and just in case yo dumb ass needed a little clarification, I was and am talkin' to yo bitch ass."

Before Zyon could even react, Yaseer had rushed him and hit him with a mean left hook. The next thing everyone saw was Yaseer and Zyon going head to head, tit for tat, like two beasts going at it in the jungle.

"Hey! Hey! Hhheeeyy!" Paris yelled out, causing the two men to pause to see what all the fuss was about. Looking at Paris' face, Yaseer knew he had just fucked up.

"Y'all are in my muhfuckin' room, my *hospital* room at that, acting like you're damn five! I just had two whole live babies and Brooklyn just died and y'all over here fighting over petty shit that, as grown men, you should be able to discuss without it going to blows. You know what? As a matter of fact, get the fuck up outta my room! The rest of y'all can stay but, Yaseer, you and Zyon gotta get the fuck out ASAP!"

"But-" Yaseer began to plead his case but was stopped with the palm of Paris' hand facing his face, along with a head shake, saying that she didn't even wanna hear it. She had seen and heard enough for one day. They had overstayed their welcome and it was past time for them to go.

Paris made her way back to her hospital bed, not even bothering to look back as Yaseer and Zyon took their walk of shame to the exit. Yaseer felt like a little ass kid who had just gotten scolded by his momma for sticking his hand in the cookie jar. He didn't know what had come over him to even let it get to blows with Zyon. Yaseer shook his head as he berated himself for acting so childish as he made his way down the hospital halls with a mournful look on his face. His emotions were everywhere and he was kinda glad Paris had kicked him out of her room. He needed time to clear his head and get his mind right. He continued his journey down the hall until he came to the baby nursery. He looked on through the window at his beautiful baby boys. His heart swelled with pride, looking down at their handsome faces through the glass window.

"Wooo wwweeee, lil man look just like you. He got yo big ass head and all," Zyon taunted from beside him.

Yaseer had been in his thoughts so much so that he forgot all about Zyon and didn't even realize that he had even followed him. Yasser shook his head with a smile on his face before responding with a smart retort of his own. "This big ass head had more girls than you did, though!"

"Negro, please, you know I had all the shorties running around the streets like ducks with their heads cut off looking for me. *Omg, where's Zyon? Have you seen Zyon? Bitch, that's my man? Is Zyon home?*" Zyon mocked in a high pitched voice as he reflected back on when he was running the streets heavy and bagging every bad female he saw.

"And even with all the shorties you had knocking on the door, you still wasn't fucking wit my numbers, though. I remember before moms and pops had got knocked, moms was blasting on my ass one day 'cause mad females kept coming to the door looking for me," Yaseer replied. Zyon laughed as he thought about the fond memory.

"Hellz yea, I remember that shit," Zyon responded as he covered his mouth with his fist to stifle a laugh. "Yyyooo, that was the day shorty came over to the house wilding 'cause she had called and thought mommy was lying about you being there. Her ass was brave as hell thinking she was about to roll up on mommy talking reckless. Ma two pieced her ass real quick. What was shorty name? Wasn't it Beatrice or some shit like that?" Zyon questioned as he laughed at the memory.

"Hell yeah, that's that crazy ass hoe name. She had the wrong one for that bullshit."

"She for damn sure did. You know sum, yo ass always messing with some crazy ass broads. You can have dem bitches all day. I'll take the few lil hunnies over all dem crazy hephas any day," Zyon said with a smirk on his face as he shook his head, reflecting back on how he and his brother used to be with the ladies back in the day.

"I feel ya on dat, bruh."

"Welp, at least wifey not cray-cray."

"That's what you think," Yaseer said with a smile, thinking of the woman who had his heart in a vice grip.

"So listen, you really think moms was lying, though? I know I snapped back there, but I mean, it's mom. She just getting out, and boom here you go accusing her of lying about something that she really may not have had a clue about," Zyon spat with malice in his voice.

Yaseer turned his back to Zyon, inhaled a deep breath, and then exhaled as he rubbed his hands down his face, before turning back around to face his younger twin.

"Yes, Zyon, I honestly think that she was lying. Come on, man, what chick that's a real rida for her man don't know the bullshit he does. How you know about one and not the other, yet they were born at the same damn time? Fuck outta here. She may not have known about it at the beginning, but through the years, she had to find out. Kids don't stay secret for too long," responded Yaseer.

"True dat, but the question is if she is lying, then why the hell she lying fo'?" Zyon questioned.

"That's the same shit I'm wondering, too," Yaseer replied with a smug look on his face. "Fuck all this wondering shit. Let's go do what we do best."

"And what's that?" Zyon questioned.

"Do you really have to even ask? We gone kill whoever and whatever we need to get answers. As of right now, ion trust no one, especially after that bullshit that happened with Ezra."

"I feel ya, bruh," Zyon stated as they began to walk back towards Paris' room.

The two brothers walked in silence, thinking of the blood, torture, and tears they would cause once more on the mean streets of Charlotte, North Carolina. Once they reached Paris' room, they both looked at each other, knowing they owed her, as well as the crew, an apology, but both knowing Paris was about to give them hell as soon as they stepped through the door. Yaseer took a deep breath before he pushed Paris' hospital room door open.

Chapter 11

Yaseer turned slightly back to Zyon and placed an index finger over his lip to silence Zyon after stepping in the door to see that Paris was sound asleep. Yaseer walked over to her and gave her a kiss on the forehead, rubbing his hand over the top of her head. She stirred slightly at the feel of his touch, then drifted back off into a deep sleep. Yaseer stared at her for a moment, watching her sleep, before nodding his head over to the direction of the door, letting Zyon know it was time to go. Yaseer turned and followed Zyon out of Paris's room.

"Alright, big bruh, where to?" Zyon questioned as they waited on the elevator.

"Shiiittt, you can either roll with me on these streets or go do you, either way don't matter to me," Yaseer replied as they stepped inside the elevator.

"Now you know I'ma ride these streets with you, ain't no question 'bout that," Zyon spat as they made their way to the first floor.

"True. Well let's ride shawty," Yaseer responded as they exited the elevator and made their way to the lobby of the hospital and out the front doors. They walked to Yaseer's blacked out 2015 Dodge Charger in silence. Yaseer unlocked the car doors and hopped inside the driver seat, followed by Zyon on the passenger side. Once they both were strapped in, Yaseer cranked his baby up, rolled the windows down, turned his music up to the max, and peeled off of Presbyterian's property. He had a lot on his brain. They had been at the hospital all day and he needed to relax. Yasser turned the music down a little so that Zyon could hear him.

"Aye, you tryna head over to Day 1 wit' me?"

"Hell yeah, you know I'm down to see some titties and ass any time."

"A'ight bet. It's a little after five. We'll swing by my crib so I can shower and change. Then we can head over there," Yaseer spat back.

"A'ight, cool beans," Zyon replied.

They rode quietly in their thoughts while the music serenaded their minds until Yaseer decided to break the quietness between them with a question he had asked himself more than once.

"Aye, Zy."

"Sup, bruh"

"You ever wondered what you would have been if you never had got in the game?"

"Nah, not really. I mean, the streets is all I know. It's what's in me. It's what's in my heart. Ion know nun else, bruh. What 'bout you?"

"I mean, at one time my thought process was just like yours, but the older I get, the more I realize the game is not it, at least not for me anymore. Now don't get me wrong, I will always have love for the game because it's the game that practically made me into the man that I am today. However, it just don't feel like me anymo'. I'm getting too old for this shit. I just wanna settle down with my family and run a little small business like the clubs, shoot, maybe even a recreation center or sum for the youngins, fam."

"I feel you on that shit, man. Maybe one day I will get tired, but I don't think it will be no time soon. I like them quick and easy dollas, and I like working when I feel like working."

"True dat, but look at the cost those quick and easy dollas come to. Shit, muhfuckas aiming at our family and our heads every day. I mean, we be beasting in these streets, but these young cats coming in the game wilding, and one day somebody will raise up and be bigger and better than we are. Shit not worth the risk anymore."

"I feel ya, man," Zyon replied with his chin in between his fingers as he looked out the window while they waited in traffic.

Yaseer turned the music back up to the max as the traffic started to finally flow. Twenty minutes later, Yaseer was pulling up to his humble abode. Yaseer pulled into his circular driveway and parked right in front of the steps that led up to his front door.

"Come on, bruh," Yaseer said in a low voice as he exited his vehicle and walked up the three little steps to his front door.

Zyon followed Yaseer inside the threshold and through the house until they stopped in the kitchen. Yaseer reached under the cabinet by the stainless steel refrigerator and grabbed a nearly half empty bottle of E&J and sat it on the black marble countertop before reaching above his forehead to grab a small crystal drinking glass.

"You want one, bruh?" Yaseer questioned as held the door to the cabinet open.

"What you drinkin', son?"

"You already know, I'm sippin' on that early Jesus," Yaseer spat.

Zyon chuckled a little before responding. "Yeah, I'll take a lil in a shot glass, please." Zyon dropped his head down, looked down at the black marble tile, and began to think of everything that had transpired in the eleven months that he had been with the crew as he waited on Yaseer to hand him his drink.

"What's on your mind, bruh?" Yaseer asked as he sat Zyon's drink down in front of him.

"Everything. You know I have been through a lot of shit, but you, my nigga, you done been through some serious shit. Gggooott damn. I'on see how you able to handle it and keep standing tall with your feet planted in the ground," Zyon spat.

"To be honest, bruh, ion even see how I'm still standing either but I refuse to let any of these muhfuckas see me weak. Ion care what they do to me or take from me, it will be a cold day in hell before they ever catch me looking like a weak lil bitch. I promise, on everything I love, I will go down fighting til my last breath."

"I feel you, bruh. Shhiittt, I'm tryna be just like you when I grow up," Zyon joked with a smile on his face as he picked up his glass and took his shot. He grimaced a little at the taste of the drink and the burn it caused as it met his chest.

"Aye, pass me that bottle. You know I gotta take a few more shots before this shit even begins to have even a little effect on me."

"Here, you ole alchy," Yaseer cracked.

"Shhhiitt, I'll be that, you ole pothead," Zyon cracked back as he watched Yaseer pull a Ziploc bag full of weed out of the coffee container that had been sitting on the counter behind them.

"I will gladly be a pothead every day of my life. Now stop running them gums and pass that bottle back this way."

"What else you got to drink on over there in that cabinet?"

"Shit, I got some hen dog, Paul Masson, Bacardi 151, Vodka, and some girly shit Paris be sippin' on called Viniq."

"Damn you holding out on a nigga. You got the good shit over there and got me over here drinking on this lil baby shit. Nigga, pass me that muhfuckin 151."

"Awww shit, yo ass bout to be tore the fuck up."

"Ya damn skippy," Zyon replied as he took the Bacardi bottle from Yaseer.

"Come on, let's go in the den and pop on the big screen," Yaseer spat as he finished rolling his blunt, grabbed his bottle, and began making his way out of the kitchen to the den.

"Aye, Zy, grab a bag of Doritos out of the pantry before you come in the den."

"Ight," Zyon replied as he grabbed his bottle, stopped by the pantry to grab the chips Yaseer had requested, and made his way to the den, as well.

"What you 'bouta put on?"

"Whatever I can find."

"Go on and toss that remote this way. Ion even know why you even got this big ass TV, knowing yo ass don't even watch TV like that."

"I know I don't, but Paris do. Plus, it's big and nice as hell so I had to cop it for my shawty."

Zyon just shook his head. "Ole pwussy whipped self," Zyon cracked.

"I'll be dat. Shit, you betta go find you a bitch and get pwussy whipped fo' yo dick stop working, muhfucka," Yaseer spat back.

"Neva dat, my ass a be in the nursing home still getting hard-ons in that bitch."

"Boy, you a fool. Well, shit, let me go hop in this good ole shower of mines and get myself presentable again so we can head on over to Day 1. You can use the shower down the hall to ya left."

"Ight bet."

Chapter 12

Yaseer walked up his circular stairway, made a right at the top of the staircase, and moseyed on down to his master bedroom. As soon as Yaseer stepped through his door, he shut and locked it behind him. Then he began stripping out of his clothes as he made his way to his massive bathroom. Yaseer brushed a hand over his head as he stepped onto the warm marble tile in his bathroom. He reached in the holder that sat beside the light switch in the bathroom and grabbed the remote to his shower. He pressed the power button to his customized shower and turned the water on. Then he used the remote to adjust the showers temperature to his liking. He replaced the remote, then reached into the same wall holder and pulled out another remote. He pointed it to the shower and powered on the Bluetooth shower speaker, then walked over to the counter where he kept his iPod docked, powered it on, connected it to the stereo, scrolled down until he found a song he liked, and then pressed play.

Yaseer stepped into the shower, bobbing his head to the sounds of Yo Gotti's song *Touchdown*. The more he listened to the song as he stood under the steaming hot water, the angrier he became, thinking about everything that had happened to him in the last year and a half. The lies, the hidden secrets, the disloyalty, the betrayal, and the hurt and pain from losing the ones he loved the most flooded his thoughts. The more he thought on everything, the harder his heart became, and the more his hand began to itch to kill something. If he didn't blow a nigga top off soon, he felt like he would lose his mind. He wanted muhfuckas in the streets the feel his pain and to realize he was the wrong one to ever cross, family or not. Betrayal was unacceptable in any way, shape, form, or fashion.

Yaseer grabbed his Tom Ford Oud Wood shower gel and wash cloth, then cleansed his body. After making sure he was good and clean, Yaseer turned the shower off, opened the shower door, and grabbed his towel off the wooden rack on the wall beside the shower. He wrapped it around his waist, then stepped onto the black rug that sat outside the shower. Yaseer ran a hand over his face, thinking about what he wanted to do after he left his club. His mind drew a blank. He didn't feel like going back up to the hospital. He knew it was a sucky thing to not wanna go back up there, but to be honest, he had been to the hospital enough times lately to last him a lifetime.

Yaseer walked to the walk-in closet in his room and pulled out a black T-shirt and some black Robin Jeans. Then he walked over to his dresser and pulled out a pair of black socks, as well as a pair of black boxer shorts and a black wife beater. Yaseer was almost done getting dressed when Zyon yelled up the stairs at him.

"Nigga, if you don't hurry yo punk ass up," Zyon shouted.

"Shut the fuck up! I got yo punk, bitch," Yaseer spat back with his voice filled with laughter.

"You and Liam worse than some broads. It ain't pose to take no nigga that long to get fuckin' dressed, wit y'all pretty asses," Zyon replied as he stepped inside of Yaseer's room.

"You just mad cause we look better than yo ugly ass," Yaseer cracked back.

"Yea, whatever. Bring ya ass," Zyon responded.

"Damn, yo ass act like you ain't neva seen ass and titties before."

"I *haven't* seen *those* hoes' ass and titties before. They new to me," Zyon replied with a chuckle.

Yaseer just shook his head at his brother with a smile on his face as he pulled his shirt over his head and made his way to the bathroom. He picked his brush up off the counter and brushed his jet black, curly hair into a neat low ponytail. He had let his hair grow out while dealing with all the bullshit that had been going on in his life. Yaseer looked at himself in the mirror, deciding that sometime within the next few days he was going to get his hair cut. He didn't wanna be looking like the rest of them young cats walking around with braids and shit.

Yaseer brushed his teeth, then gargled with mouthwash before spitting it out and washing his mouth out. He put on his Tom Ford Oud Wood deodorant, then sprayed on his Tom Ford Noir de Noir cologne. He double checked himself in the mirror before walking out into his room to his closet once more and grabbing the shoe box off of the top shelf that housed his black Timbs. Then he went to sit on the bed to put them on. Once he had his shoes on, he walked over to the nightstand beside his bed, and then to a small closet beside the bathroom. He opened it, flicked the light on, and then stepped inside. At the back of the closet was a door with a scanner that opened with a scan of his hand. Once it was opened, Yaseer stepped inside of a larger room that kind of looked like the vault inside of a jewelry store. The only thing different was, not only did it house his jewelry, it also housed his weapons, as well as a large safe that contained his money.

Yaseer walked to the wall in the back and looked over his weapons, trying to decide which weapon he wanted to carry. His eyes settled on his twin black .45's that were trimmed in gold. He grabbed his black shoulder holsters that he kept near his weapons, put it on, then grabbed both of his tools and placed one in each holster. Then he walked over to his safe, unlocked it, grabbed a stack, and then walked over to the wall near the door and grabbed one of his THT chains. He had multiple ones, since every New Year he got new ones made to celebrate their crew making it to another year and to celebrate the lives of the ones they may have lost that year. Yaseer put his chain on as he exited his vault. He shut the door behind him, making sure he heard it click before walking out of the closet.

"A'ight, bruh, leggo," Yaseer said to Zyon, who was sitting on the bed concentrating hard on his phone screen.

"Bout time, wit yo slow ass," Zyon spat as he stood up and began making his way to the door with Yaseer following close behind him. The gentlemen walked downstairs to the front door. Yaseer grabbed the keys to his all-black 2015 Dodge Charger and was more than ready to go get into some action. Yaseer tossed the keys to Zyon.

"Go and drive, fam, while I roll this shit up."

"The fuck going on here? You, out of all people, 'bout to let me drive yo whip? When da fuck yo ass start letting people get behind the wheel of yo shit? You don't never let no one drive yo shit," Zyon spat.

"I let Paris drive them," Yaseer spat back with a smirk on his face.

"Nigga, you know that shit don't even count. That's wifey right there. Try again, muhfucka."

"How that don't count? She another whole nother person than me. So that do count."

"No the fuck it don't, nigga, she just had two whole live babies by yo dumb ass."

"Yeah, whatever, it count in my book," Yaseer replied with a smile still plastered on his face.

He knew damn well that shit didn't count, he just liked fuckin' with Zyon to piss him off. Since they were kids,

Yaseer always teased and said shit to Zyon, knowing it was going to get under his skin. In his eyes, it was to help him get tougher so that words from some random nigga on the street wouldn't get to him and land his hot headed ass in jail, and up until this day, Yaseer was the only person on earth that could ever say or do something to be able get under his skin. Yaseer and Zyon opened the car doors, got inside, put their seat belts on, and peeled out with one place in mind, Day 1.

Royal Nicole

Chapter 13

"So um, Miss Ma'am, does Yaseer even know you and the boys are being released to go home?" London asked, laying across Paris' hospital bed as she watched Paris walk back and forth through the room, packing up everything that had accumulated in the hospital the last few days since the birth of the YJ and Jaseer

"Nope. I wanted it to be a surprise. I paid the doctor a hunnid bucks to tell Yaseer some bullshit about having to keep me for another forty-eight hours to monitor my blood pressure, knowing good and well my pressure has been under control since I pushed them little boogas out," Paris replied. Yaseer had pissed her off earlier, acting like a kid, but truth of the matter was that she could never stay mad at him for too long, no matter what he did. London just shook her head.

"You two are something else," London spat before getting up off of the bed to help Paris finish packing up everything that the hospital had given her.

"Don't I know it?" Paris replied back to her.

"Welp, sis, I think that's about it?" London commented about ten minutes later.

"You know what? It seem like these lil boys of mine got the damn world in here. I did not expect the hospital to give me all this shit for them. You got the car seats set up in your car already, right?" Paris asked.

"Yea, girl. You better be glad the crew left early 'cause I did not know how I was going to sneak downstairs to get them things out the back of my truck without Liam's ass following me down there."

"True. So what do you think about Erin?" Paris said as she sat down to wait for the nurses to bring her babies from the nursery.

"She seem cool, but baby girl is a little rougher around the edges than Brooklyn. They may look identical to one another, but that's where all the similarity ends at. Like, P, they act nothing alike at all. I heard 'bout how lil momma wilded out on her mans in the A when the crew went up there. Brooklyn was a lil cray-cray, but I think lil momma may have her beat," London replied.

"Um um, looks like her brothers about to have a time on their hands," Paris spat back.

"Oh yes ma'am, they are, and I'm going to enjoy watching all the hell she 'bout to put them through," London responded, thinking of the new partner in crime her and Paris had gained, but that smile quickly fell when she thought about the partner in crime they had just lost, who was like a sister to both of them.

"Well, let me page those nurses to see where they are at with my babies," Paris stated as she got up and made her way to her hospital bed so that she could press the call light.

"Can we help you?" a nurse answered.

"Yes, I just wanted to know how much longer it would be before you all bring my sons to me so that we can leave."

"They're on the way to you now."

"Ok, thanks, hun," Paris responded.

As soon as she put the call light down and went to turn to go sit back down, she heard the door open. In walked two nurses, pushing her handsome newborn sons. Paris and London rushed to the boys' side. They were both eager to hold them. London looked down at YJ, and for just a brief moment, wondered what it would be like if her and Liam had a seed together. Never in her life did she think she would ever want to be a mom because she was always on the move, grinding. But now, looking down at baby YJ, her whole outlook on becoming a mother was beginning to change. Maybe she could slow down now. She had more than enough money to chill with for a long, long time. Maybe she could open the weave Salon that she had always dreamed of since she was a child. She pondered while transferring YJ from the cradled position she had him onto her shoulder.

"What you over there thinking about, sis?"

London was a little hesitant to verbalize what was on her mind to her big sister, but figured maybe Paris could give her some sound advice. She exhaled before going on to tell Paris what she had previously been thinking. Paris listened to every single word that came out of London's mouth. She was proud to see that her sister was beginning to mature. She waited for London to finish talking before she voiced her opinion.

"Sis, we had been living the street life for a very long time before we even met the boys, and after a while, we all have to grow up. No one lasts in this life forever without there being dire consequences. Maybe it is time for you to act on your dreams and go legit. I am more than sure that Yaseer would understand."

"Hope you're right, sis," London said as she picked up YJ's baby bag.

"I know I am. Now come on so you can go find my brother-in-law and go half on me some nieces and nephews that I can spoil," Paris spat with a smirk on her face.

"Come on, heffa, with yo nasty mouth," London spat back, smiling at her big sister.

***

A little over two hours later, the twins were settled in their new rooms and Paris was in the kitchen whipping up a meal to surprise Yaseer with. She was making his favorite meal for him, BBQ chicken, collard greens, and baked mac and cheese, with cornbread, and for dessert, she had banana pudding. She couldn't wait to walk into his office with his favorites and see him go ham over his food. No more than thirty minutes later, everything was done. She placed healthy portions of everything into Tupperware bowls and packed them in a big black and gold Gucci hand bag before walking into the living room and grabbing her slide-ons.

"Aye, L. L, London!" Paris called out to her sister who had fallen sound asleep on the couch watching Law & Order: SVU.

"Yeah," London said in a sleep filled voice as she sat up and looked at Paris.

"I'm 'bout to go drop some food off to Yaseer. You good here with the twins until I get back?"

London looked at Paris as if she had just grown two heads before responding.

"Girl, bye. Did you just really ask me some bullshit like that? You know I'm good here with these babies."

"Well, hell, I still had to ask. I don't want you thinking I'm just leaving them off on you."

"Bye, Paris, and hurry up and get ya ass back here 'cause you know you don't have any business being out anywhere after just giving birth. You got one hour to get there and back before I call Yaseer on ya ass!"

"Alright, alright, you act like I'm going to the store or something. Damn, man. Alright, heffa, I'm out, be back soon," Paris shouted as she walked out of the living room and to the door.

Nightfall had begun to bless the earth's atmosphere just as Paris pulled up to Day 1. The time on the dashboard read 7:57pm. She knew Yaseer was probably sitting at his desk going over the club's books. A smile crept over her face as she got out of the car with her bags of food in tow and made her way to the entrance of the club. She nodded to the security guard known as Rome and continued on through the club's entrance.

Once inside, she walked upstairs and made a left at the top of the stairs to go down the hallway that led to Yaseer's office. She was almost to his office when she spotted one of the strippers she knew as Cutie Pie walking down the hallway towards her. She liked Cutie. Unlike some of the other strip hoes in the club, Cutie never caused any problems. Paris had only talked to her a few times, and from what she had gathered, Cutie was out here trying to get money to take care of her son, bills at home, and college tuition that her financial aid didn't cover. When her set was up, she didn't stick around to mingle, she got her shit and got ghost. Paris made a mental note to sit down and have lunch with her one day, hoping that she may be able to interest her into getting into another line of work if she got her the job.

"Hi, hun, how you doing today?" Paris asked as they got closer to one another.

"I'm alright, just tryna get myself together for this set," Cutie answered as she reached out to give Paris a hug.

"I feel ya on that, ma. Listen, take my personal number down and give me a call when you're free. I got a business opportunity for you that I think you will find more satisfying than taking off ya clothes for these thirsty ass niggas."

"A'ight bet. I'll reach out once I finish up here for to-night," Cutie answered with a smile full of bliss plastered on her beautiful cinnamon colored face. Then she proceeded on to finish getting ready.

Paris continued on her journey to Yaseer's office. She knocked lightly before opening the door. She damn near dropped everything she had in her hand when her eyes landed on a bitch's head in her man's lap while he had his head leaned back on his chair with his left hand on the back of the stripper's head. He was so caught up in the moment that he didn't even realize that the door had even been opened, let alone that anyone was watching. It took everything within Paris not to go ape shit. She took in a deep breath before letting herself be known.

Chapter 14

"Damn, bitch, relax dat throat a lil bit. Over there gagging and shit like you'on know how to take a dick down the throat like a good hoe. Hell, if you gone do my job, at least make sure you gone do the shit right, or better," Paris stated as she walked into Yaseer's office and placed the food she had made for him on his desk.

Yaseer damn near jumped out of his skin when he realized Paris had just caught him with his dick in someone else's mouth. The smile that graced her face looked like she didn't care, well at least that was how it looked to Sasha, the stripper that was still on her knees with the Kelly Bundy dumb look on her face, watching the live show between her boss and his girl like it was Love and Hip Hop or something. But Yaseer knew better. The smile on her face was the one that graced a true killa's face before they went in for the kill. If Sasha knew like he knew, she would get out of dodge before her brains hit the fan.

"Ohh, I see you one of them brave hoes that don't know how to take a hint. Okay, stay right there," Paris spat as she reached to the small of her back and pulled her purple baby ratchet that she had nicknamed Royal from behind her and cocked it. Before she could finish cocking it, Sasha was on her feet and running towards the door, trying to get the hell out of dodge. She didn't want them type of problems.

"Oh, don't run now," Paris yelled as she turned and fired a round off in Sasha's direction.

The bullet missed Sasha by a hair. Paris turned back in Yaseer's direction with her hammer still in her hand, business end pointed to the floor. Paris smiled, showing all thirty-two teeth as she dropped her head down towards her chest, then looked back at Yaseer. For a minute, they both sat staring at each other before Paris made up in her mind what she wanted to do. Yaseer did not want to move an inch, in fear of what Paris might do if he did. Paris replaced her gun back in the small of her back, then looked down at her ring finger on her left hand and gazed at the engagement ring that she used to proudly wear. She looked at it for a second longer before taking it off and placing it on the end of Yaseer's desk and turning to walk away. She had no words for Yaseer. She knew he was hurting inside, but that didn't give him a pass to hurt her. He had done that more than enough in the time that they had been together and she refused to take that any longer.

Finally realizing what was happening, Yaseer hurriedly fixed himself and jumped to his feet, chasing behind her.

"Paris! Paris," Yaseer called out to no avail. Paris already had her hand on the door knob and had barely gotten it open before Yaseer reached above her and slammed it closed.

"Yaseer, move. Just please move," Paris pleaded.

"No. I can't. I can't lose you, too, Paris," Yaseer begged as he wrapped his arms around her waist real tight and pulled her to him. As much as it felt good to have his arms wrapped around her, she had to stand her ground in order to save her heart from any further damage.

"Are you that damn blind to where you can't see that you have already lost me? Ain't no backsies after that, Yaseer. Like, I'm done for real. Go on. You made your bed, now lie in it," Paris spewed out as she went to try to move out of his warm embrace.

Yaseer held her tighter, refusing to believe that she was done with him.

"Come on, baby, it's me you talking to. Don't say you done, don't tell me I've lost you. I promise I'll lose it if you walk out this door. I swear, I didn't mean for this to happen.

I was drinking and I kept thinking about Brooklyn and I just wanted the pain to stop and you weren't here."

"Pow!" Before Yaseer could even finish what he was saying, Paris had turned around and smacked the fire out of him, causing him to stumble a little bit.

"Nigga, I just got done giving birth to not one, but *two* of your babies, and you gone spit that lame ass bullshit about me not being here as a reason for you to stick your dick in dat baldheaded hoe's mouth? Fuck you!" Paris screamed as she ran up on Yaseer swinging blow after blow, hitting him anywhere that she could land a hit. Face, shoulder, chest, stomach, it didn't matter as long as her fist connected with a body part.

"Alright, Paris, that's enough. Paris! I said that's enough," Yaseer spat as he grabbed her fists to try and restrain her. But Paris wasn't tryna hear that, she kept swinging, thinking it wouldn't be enough until she felt like it was enough.

"No! No! You don't get to tell me what's enough! You don't get that option! Was it enough when you let me go to prison for you? Was it enough when you cheated on me and had them babies with that stupid bitch while I was serving your time? Was it enough when Ezra raped me behind yo bullshit and because of my affiliation with you? Was it enough when you just had that hoe's mouth wrapped around your dick after I just had kids for you? Was it *enough* then?" Paris screamed in between any hit she could get in as tears dripped down her pretty face.

Yaseer used all the strength he had to grab and restrain her, and then pull her towards his chest. Paris continued trying to hit Yaseer's chest as she cried and he held her in a tight embrace until all she could do was cry. She'd had enough and her heart was truly broken in pieces. She couldn't understand why she wasn't enough for Yaseer. It should have been her he turned to in his time of need, not some random thot bucket. A lone tear ran down Yaseer's face. He couldn't stand to see her hurting and crying, especially since he was the person who was behind some of the pain on her face.

"I'm so, so sorry, P. I swear, I am. I just wanted the pain to stop. I just wanted to get my brain off of Brooklyn. I just wanted the pain to stop," Yaseer said as he finally broke down crying for the first time since Brooklyn had died. Her funeral was two days away and he was falling apart. Yaseer cried harder than he ever had before as he began falling to his knees in tears. He could no longer hold everything inside as he was used to doing. It was too much for him to bear.

"Please don't leave me. I need you, P. I can't do this without you. I just can't," Yaseer pleaded quietly in between sobs as he held Paris around her legs with his head resting on her thighs. Paris got down on her knees and wrapped her arms around him. Seeing Yaseer cry was like seeing a shooting star. It was very rare. So to see him like this pulled at her heart strings more than ever.

"Ssshhh, it's ok, bae, it's ok. I'm here, love," Paris quietly said as she put her petite hand behind his head and brought it down to her chest and held him there as he cried his soul out. She leaned her head down on top of his as he continued to cry.

Once his sobs started to slow down, she began to stand, pulling him up along with her. "Come on, let's go lay down. I think we have had enough for one day," Paris said as she pulled him towards the mini bedroom that he had in his office.

Paris sat on the side of the bed and removed her shoes. Then she laid down on the bed, followed by Yaseer. He wrapped his arm around her and pulled her close. A tear slipped out of the corner of Paris' eye onto the pillow as she thought about everything she had unnecessarily been through because of the love, loyalty, and respect she had for Yaseer. She looked back at Yaseer and, as bad as she felt for him because he had loss his baby sister, she couldn't help but feel some resentment towards him for all the trouble he had caused in her life. Knowing he was sound asleep, Paris sat up, put her shoes on, walked out the room, grabbed her purse, and quietly left his office, making sure to lock the door behind herself. Paris swiped another tear as it fell down her face. She refused to let these stripper hoes see her crying and weak, no matter how bad her heart was hurting. Paris reached in her purse and grabbed her oversized Chanel sunglasses and slid them on her face as she walked down the hall of Day 1 leading to the exit door.

Chapter 15

Paris walked out of Day 1 with one thing in her mind that she knew for sure. At that moment, she was done with Yaseer and she would be done with him until she made him feel the same exact pain that she had in her heart at that very moment. Sure, she would let him grieve for now. But after the grieving period was over, it would be on and popping.

Paris got in her car and sat there for a minute before cranking it up and pulling off. She turned up Beyoncé's song *Jealous* as she drove out of the parking lot. Instead of going in the direction of home, she decided to hop on Independence Highway and just drive and let YouTube Red be her DJ as she drove down the dark highways of Charlotte, North Carolina. She looked at downtown Charlotte, and then the Panthers' stadium as she drove. Track after track played as she continued driving. After stopping to get some snacks and turning back in the opposite direction, she was back on the highway, reaching her unintended destination almost four hours later.

Getting out of her car, she went and knocked on a door that she hadn't knocked on in a long time. An old friend that she'd known since she was a youngin' but had fell back from once she started messing with Yaseer. He was one the only person besides Yaseer and her sister that kept money on her books when she was on lock. That was the one thing she dared not to mention to Yaseer. He would have flipped out if he found out another nigga was putting money on her books, other than him.

"Knock, Knock, Knock." Paris knew it was late and she should have called before driving all the way down to Raleigh, North Carolina. To be honest, she hadn't even planned on driving there but it was where her car and heart

led her and on his doorstep is where she landed. Paris waited for a few seconds before turning around to leave. She knew she shouldn't have gone there. It was a huge mistake. She was almost to her car when she heard his voice call her name.

"*Paris?*"

"Omg! Seven!" Paris exclaimed as she ran into his arms.

"Hey to you, too! What yo yella ass doing down here at damn near 3:30 in the morning?"

"Ooohh nothing, I was just in the neighborhood," Paris said with a smile on her face.

"Nigga, who ya ass think you fooling with that wack ass line? Get oonn in here, shawty. What's really good with ya?" he asked as he stepped back to let her inside before shutting and locking the door behind them.

Paris stood off to the side so that Seven could get in front of her and lead the way through his mini mansion to the living room.

"Go on and sit down in there. Give me a few minutes and you will have my full, undivided attention, ma'am."

Paris walked into the living room and sat down. She admired his living room. It had that homey feel to it. Maybe because it was a one story brick house. She'd always loved brick houses. They felt just how his felt. Homey. She sat back and began looking at the pictures that he had on his mantel and her eyes fell on one in particular. It was a picture that his grams had taken of them playfully smiling when they were no more than 10 years old. She got up, walked over and picked up the photo. *Oh how it was so much easier being a child,* she thought to herself as Seven walked back into the room carrying a tray with food snacks on it.

"The hell, Sev," Paris mumbled to herself as she walked over to where he was.

She couldn't help but smile. After all these years, he still remembered her favorite snacks. She was surprised that he even kept them in stock at his house. He had everything just right. He had mini strawberry bagels with berry cream cheese on them, a pint of cookies and cream ice cream, some ranch Doritos, and a peach soda. He was only missing one thing on the tray, but she wasn't even bothered by that because he had remembered everything else.

"Up, hold on, I forgot something," he said as he walked out of the room and came back with a small Ziploc bag that contained her all-time favorite, blue peanut M&M's. She dang near snatched them out of his hand when she saw him coming towards her with them.

"Omg, Sev, I can't believe that you remember all of my favorite snacks. Let me find out you becoming a foodie like me!" Paris cracked with a smile on her face as she took out a hand full of M&M's and started popping them into her mouth, one by one, back to back.

"So what's up, shawty? What's really good with ya?" Seven said as he sat down on the couch and patted the spot beside him for her to sit down.

For a minute, Paris had forgotten all of her problems and why she had even come there in the first place. But now, thinking back at what had driven her to come all the way to his house had her starting to feel sad and pissed at the same time. She exhaled deeply as she sat down beside him.

"Well, to make a long story short, I'm tired of dealing with all the fuckery Yaseer keeps putting me through. Like, I am so tired of the bullshit. Like, I am literally at the point to where I have reached my limit. Like, there is only so much a person can take and I have taken all that I can, plus some.'

"Aww hell. His black ass must've cheated."

Paris couldn't help but to laugh at the way he said it. "Aww hell is right! Yeah, I did just catch him cheating on me, but a bitch giving him sloppy toppy is not even what is pissing me off the most. Like, dude, I just gave whole live birth to our babies, his baby sister just died during birth, and on top of everything, I have been through hell with his ass from doing his time to getting raped for being loyal to his dumb ass. He had babies on me with a hoe while I was on lock. Like, I am ssssoooo over him. How the hell can you claim to love someone when you keep doing them dirty over and over again? Like, I'm just tired. I-I just can't deal with that now. Anywho, enough about me, what's been going on with you? How you been?"

"None much, really, same ole, same ole. Just chilling and making money.'

"I hear that. So how things going with you and Shauny?"

"They not."

"Man, get the fuck outta here. Y'all niggas been going at it for damn near thirty years."

"Ha, ha, shut up, ninja, I ain't even thirty yet, goofball," Seven replied with a smirk on his face. "So how's is everything with Aunt Debbie? It's been awhile since I've caught up with you, and you know I love yo auntie like a fat kid love cake," Seven asked.

"Yea right, you only love her for her cooking, but umm it's been a hot minute since I've talked to her. You know she don't fool with me much anymore because she still doesn't approve of Yaseer. She feels like he ruined me. London talks to her all the time, though, so I know she's alright in life."

"Damn, that's crazy, son, but I can understand her point of view. Everyone wants their child, or the child they have raised, to end up on the right side of the track. However, I don't approve of her methods of falling back from you, I do completely understand her reasoning."

"True. It is what it is. It's whateva. I've come to just accept it."

"I feel you. So how long you plan to be down here?"

"Hell, prolly til Saturday. That's when Brooklyn's funeral is and I can't miss that for nothing in the world. Speaking of funerals, come with me outside and stand guard while I get this tracking device off my car 'fore someone be planning another funeral."

"Ha. Imagine that. Come on, wit yo scary ass."

"Oh, don't get it twisted, I'm far from scary, my dude. I stay packing. I just need you to make sure don't nobody roll up on a shawty while I'm under my car."

"Yeah alright, if you say so," Seven spat back as he slipped on his Nike slide-ons and followed Paris outside to her car.

Chapter 16

"Got it," Seven said as he came from under Paris's Charger.

"You do know that I could have done that, right?" Paris spat.

"Yeah, you could have, but what kind of man would I be to sit back and let you do something of the sort? Only bitch made niggas do that, ma."

"Uh oh, uh oh, let me find out you a whole live gentleman," Paris cracked.

"I been one. Yo ass just blind to it," Seven cracked back.

"If you say so," Paris spat, brushing off his comment. Truth was she knew he was right. She knew he used to have a thing for her when they were younger. But he was never gutta enough for her. Like, he was a little too good, and she didn't know how to handle that, so she felt it was better that they remained friends and that's what they had been up until now. Paris looked over her shoulder then back at Seven, who was now standing at his full height in front of her. Paris looked up into his gorgeous face. He was the total opposite of Yaseer. On the outside, he looked like another dude from the hood. He stood at six foot two. He had some muscles but he was slim and brown skin. He kind of reminded her of the actor Kofi Siriboe, trimmed down beard and all. However, even though he was from the hood, you could never tell unless you pissed him off. He was actually a very intelligent guy. He got out of the streets, went back to school, got his bachelor's and was now a successful appraiser of Commercial Real Estate.

"So what you tryna do with this tracker?" Seven asked Paris, looking down into her beautiful caramel face.

"Oh, umm, I gotta find somewhere to toss it just in case Yaseer tries to come looking for me. And I need to let my sister know that I'm alright so she don't be sitting there pulling out her hair, worrying about me," Paris said as Seven broke her out of her train of thought. She was actually glad he had done that because she had no business thinking of Seven as anything other than a friend, no matter how cute he was.

"Let me grab my keys and I know the perfect place to go toss it. I'll drive and you can hit lil ma up."

"Sounds like a plan. Leggo," Paris said as she walked over to Seven's all-white 2015 Dodge Ram 1500. As soon as she got to the passenger side, Seven was locking the front door and making his way to the car. He pressed the unlock button on his keyless entry car remote as he walked over to the car so that Paris could go ahead and get.

"You and these damn pickup trucks," Paris cracked once Seven got inside the car.

"Hole up now, you not 'bout to start hating on my baby like that."

"Ain't nobody hating on yo damn baby. All I'm saying is you're literally the only nigga I know that damn near has an obsession with these things."

"Good! Ion want nobody else tryna be like me, and I don't wanna be caught tryna be like no one else, ya dig."

"I can respect that," Paris replied as she pulled out her iPhone 6 plus to call London. She put the phone to her ear and waited to be greeted by a worried London on the other end.

"Where the hell yo yella ass at?" London answered in a much calmer voice than Paris anticipated.

"I caught Yaseer's dumb ass cheating, yet again. I guess he got amnesia or something because his black ass must have forgotten that he had a whole live fiancé, not to mention all the shit we had went through because of Ariel's unstable ass.

I just, I just can't handle being around him right now, L, especially with everything that just happened with Brooklyn, Erin coming into the picture, and Seer's mom's getting out. I'm with Sev so I'm good," Paris replied.

"OMG! You're with Seven! Oh my God, I haven't seen him in forever. Like, I was mad young the last time I saw him. Let me speak to him," London spat out excitedly. Paris shook her head as she pulled the phone from her ear and held the phone out to him. She could do nothing, but smile at her baby sister's shenanigans.

"Sup, girl," Seven responded as he put the phone to his ear.

"Look what the wind blew in, how you been, ole timer?" London replied.

"Up, see, there you go, already starting with them old jokes. I ain't that much older than yo little short ass, but anyways, I been good, lil girl," Seven cracked.

"Haha, you ain't funny, wit yo black ass. Anywho, how you and my sis link up? I didn't even know you guys were still in contact with one another. You know what? Never mind, just take care of my sister, ninja, and tell her the babies are good. Gotta go," London spat and hung up the phone without another word. Seven pulled the phone from his ear, looked at it, and shook his head.

"Well, it seems like baby sis was in a rush to get off the phone. Hope everything is alright," Seven said in a concerned voice as he passed the phone to Paris.

"I'm sure everything is alright. If I know her like I'm sure I do, then either Liam or Yaseer just came in the house."

"Oh, and she told me to tell you that the babies were good," Seven said as they pulled up to a deserted parking lot. Looking out, you could see a big body of water. It was very beautiful.

"Where we at, Sev?"

"Lake Johnson Park. When Sade comes down to visit and brings Choc and Vanilla with her, this is where we bring them to let them run that energy off. It's a must before them muts step there paws inside of my house. Them mugs be hype as hell when they get out the damn car," Seven said as he got out and started walking towards the lake. Paris got out and followed closely behind him.

"Well, damn, I know where to toss my ratchet if I ever gotta body a nigga down here," Paris cracked as they reached the massive body of water.

"Yea a'ight, killa," Seven responded as he tossed the tracker in the water.

"A'ight, come on, shawty," he said as he turned back around to walk to his truck. Once again, Paris followed him.

"So do you think London was able to handle Yaseer and his brother?" Seven asked as they got back in his truck.

"Ooohh, I'm sure Yaseer or Liam is probably wishing they hadn't even stepped foot in the house by now," Paris said with a smirk on her face, knowing without a shadow of a doubt that Yaseer was getting his whole life handed to him by now.

Chapter 17

"Y'all got your nerve walking in this house at damn near six in the fuckin' morning!" London fussed as Yaseer walked in the house, followed by Liam.

"Look, L, I ain't tryna hear all that rah-rah this early in the damn morning," Yaseer spat as he walked past London and went upstairs. London started to pop back at him with something smart, but she decided to wait. She looked down at her wristwatch and gave him no less than a minute before he came storming back down the stairs. A smirk came over her face as she waited.

"Why yo ass not home in the bed sleep?" Liam questioned as he walked up on London and pulled her into an embrace.

"Same reason yo ass not home in the bed sleep," London spat back.

"Alright, now, with yo smart ass," Liam quipped as he reached down and smacked her on the butt.

"Yea, yea," London popped back as she heard Yaseer coming down the stairs. She turned in Liam's arms and relaxed as she waited to hear the question she knew Yaseer was about to ask.

"Aye, where Paris at, L?"

"Hell if I know. She a grown ass woman. I don't keep tabs on her. Go ask that lil boppa who you was cheating with," London spat back with venom dripping off the end of her comment. The little sweet smirk that she had just had on her face had turned into a full scowl. She was mean muggin' the hell out of Yaseer. If looks could kill, Yaseer would be straight massacred with no remains left to identify the body.

"Oohh shit," Liam muttered under his breath.

"Man, I ain't got time for the bullshit, L. I know yo ass know where the fuck she at," Yaseer replied with his voice raising a little.

"You know what? I do. But I ain't tellin' yo dog ass shit," London spat back as she broke out of Liam's embrace ready for whatever.

"Who da fuck you raising up on like you gon' do some, shawty?" Yaseer yelled as he stepped to London.

Liam moved up a little. He was trying to stay out of it, but Yaseer was starting to take it a little too far for his comfort.

"I'm talking to yo stupid ass!" London yelled back as she stepped toe to toe with Yaseer. Unlike everybody else, she was far from scared of Yaseer. Not one man on earth put fear in her heart. The only one thing that scared her in life was losing her family to death.

"Who in the hell you think you talking to?" Yaseer spat as he wrapped his massive hand around her neck lightning fast. Before London could pull her piece from her hip, Yaseer went flying across the room.

"Da fuck yo problem, bruh? Have you lost yo fuckin' mind?" Liam yelled as he walked over to Yaseer and punched him dead in his jaw, knocking him off balance before he could stand back to his full height. Hearing a gun being cocked back got Yaseer's senses to come back immediately. Looking up at Liam, he came face to face with the business end of Liam's .45.

"Don't you ever in yo fuckin' life put yo hands on my wife, unless you ready to go say hello to Ezra in hell. Ion give a fuck what you and Paris go through, don't let dat shit cost you yo life, bruh," Liam threatened before putting his gun back in his gun holster and walking away, leaving

Yaseer sitting there in shock that his baby brother had literally just boss'd up on him and put him in check.

"Get yo shit together and let's go, London, before I put a bullet in this nigga behind you. Oh and by the way, Erin dropped the girls off late last night. They are in their room asleep, just in case you were wondering.," Liam said as he made his way to the door. London quickly gathered her things and was out the door in a flash.

***

Yaseer wiped the side of his mouth as he picked up the things that had fallen on the floor. Hearing the sound of crying, Yaseer frowned up his face, walked down the hallway, and peeped in the room that they had set up for the boys. Low and behold, Yaseer Jr. was in there screaming his head off. Yaseer walked over to the wooden crib, bent down, and picked the newborn infant up, placing him on his shoulder. He began patting his back as he walked over to the changing table to see if he needed to be changed.

"Sup, little man," Yaseer said in a soft voice as he looked down at his son who was now wide awake. Yaseer looked in his diaper and frowned up his face. He would never understand how something so cute could push something out of it that smelled so foul.

"Gotdamn, lil man, what the hell yo aunt London done fed yo lil ass?" Yaseer mumbled under his breath as he grabbed the items he needed to change YJ's pamper. He frowned up his face once again as he went through the process of changing his son's diaper. Once he had YJ's night pants back on him, he picked him up, along with the dirty diaper, and walked over to the diaper genie to dispose of it. Then he walked over to Jaseer's crib, who was sleeping peacefully. Yaseer bent over and pulled Jaseer's covers up on him, then walked out of the room carrying YJ. He walked down to the girl's room to see if they were still asleep. He peeped his head in, and sure nuff, they were in there beds knocked out.

After making sure they were okay, Yaseer walked up the hallway to the kitchen, grabbed a bottle out of the refrigerator, sat it on the counter, and reached over and turned the bottle warmer on. He placed the bottle in the warmer and waited for it to ding to say it was done. It wasn't long before it rang. Yaseer grabbed the bottle and walked out of the kitchen to the den and sat down in his chair. He repositioned YJ to where he was cradling him in the bend of his arm. He switched the bottle to his other hand and then proceeded to test the bottle on his arm to make sure it wasn't too hot. The temperature was just right. Yaseer leaned back as he put the bottle to the eager baby's lips.

"I see you gone be a night owl just like yo momma," Yaseer said as he looked down at YJ, who now had his eyes closed with his little fists balled up on each side of his face as he sucked the bottle. Yaseer lightly bounced his leg up and down as YJ ate. He leaned his head back on the chair and closed his eyes as he imagined what was going through Paris mind and where she could be right now. He was about two point nine seconds away from sending his goons out to look for her. He just hoped and prayed that wherever Paris was, she was safe.

Chapter 18

Paris felt the warm even breath of Seven on her face. She sat up in his arms with sleep filled eyes and looked around. It was way past time for her to get back home. It was Friday morning, the day before Brooklyn's funeral, and she needed to get back home so that she could get prepared for tomorrow, as well as be there for her friends and family in this time of grief as they prepared to send their sister off. Paris spotted her jacket on the armrest of the loveseat, as well as her shoes right beside it. She was glad that everything was all in one place. She just wanted to grab her things, get back on the road, and get things over and done, including the arguing she knew that her and Yaseer were bound to do as soon as she docked the doorstep to their humble abode. Leaning up, she tapped Seven lightly on his shoulder, causing him to stir just a little but not enough to fully awaken him.

"Seven... Sev..." she called out slightly above a whisper as she continued to lightly tap him. Seven's eyes finally opened slightly and a small smile crept upon his lips.

"Morning, beautiful," he said in a sleep filled voice as he took his hand and rubbed the side of her face, then let it drop to his lap.

"Morning, handsome. I just wanted to let you know that I was about to leave so that you can lock up. Don't need nobody running up on you in yo crib," Paris cracked as she got up and walked over to gather her belongings.

"Girl, bye. You know better than anyone that. Ya boy stay with that thang ready," Seven said as he reached on the side of the couch between the end table and pulled out a .357 Magnum and placed it on his lap.

"I plays no games, baby girl," he spat as he once again picked the weapon up and placed it back in its proper spot.

"Yeah, ok," Paris said as she slipped her arms in her jacket and prepared to leave. "Well, Seven, it was nice catching up with ya, but it's time for me to head on out. We will have to do this again soon, babes."

"Dats what it do, ma. I'll catch you later," Seven said as he and Paris embraced. Paris reached up on her tippy toes and gave him a kiss on the cheek, then proceeded out the door. Seven leaned on the door frame as he watched Paris leave. Once she was in the car, she looked up at Seven standing in the doorway and smiled as she began backing out of the driveway. She couldn't help but to laugh when he put his hand up to his ear like a phone and mouthed call me with a big grin on his face. He had always been a bit of a goofball since she had known him.

Paris leaned her head back on her headrest as she drove down the highway back home, thinking about the argument she was sure she was about to have with Yaseer about where she had been. She shook her head. She was more than ready to do battle with him right about now. Before Paris knew it, she was pulling up to the building she once looked at as her home. Now it just seemed like a house that she stayed in. There was a big difference, in her book, between a house and a home. Exhaling deeply, she unbuckled her seatbelt, exited her vehicle, and made her way to the front door. She inhaled deeply and then exhaled one more time before unlocking and opening the door. Stepping inside, she stopped in her tracks when she heard the beautiful sounds of Dru Hill playing throughout the house.

"Girl, I know that things aren't going right, but don't you think it deserves a fight? A love like ours don't happen every day. And we're losing it right as we speak. And if we don't

wake up, it's a memory. A time gone past, a love that sailed away. But we're not making love no more. We're not even trying to change. Tell me how it slips away. Does it ever stay the same? We don't even talk no more. We've ran out of words to say. Tell me it don't have to change. Won't it ever stay the same? I dream of lovers past and I see a girl so sad 'cause she lost the only man she loved. He went away. Well it's not too late for us to change."

Paris slowly walked through the house to find where the music was coming from. The closer she got to the music, she could hear Yaseer singing along with the lyrics. She smiled to herself as she listened to him sing. At one time in her life, hearing him sing would've damn near drenched her panties, it still did when she wasn't pissed at him like she was now. Right about now, she just wanted to beat the hell out of him for being stupid and for being the one person who was single handedly taking her soul from her and making her heart cold. She knew he was sorry and going through some real emotional shit with losing his sister and all, but that still gave him no excuse to treat her any kind of way because she would never do that to him if the shoe was on the other foot. Paris walked into the kitchen and saw Yaseer sitting on a stool at the island with a bottle of Henny and a glass half full in his hand. She leaned back and watched as he held the drink and continued to sing the rest of the lyrics to *We're Not Making Love No More.* She stood there quietly as the song ended and *Confessions Part Two* by Usher began. That was when she could no longer keep silent and decided to make her presence known.

"Yeah, a'ight, you bet not have not nan nother bitch pregnant, or I swear fo M&M's my bullets won't miss next time. You got me?" Paris said as she walked up beside Yaseer.

Yaseer damn near jumped out of his skin and almost pulled his piece out until he realized it was Paris. He was so in his feelings, drowning in his sorrow, that he hadn't even been paying attention, thus the reason he didn't even realize that Paris had even arrived, let alone entered the house. Seeing that it was just Paris, Yaseer placed his piece back on the island, stood up, turned fully to Paris, looked at her for a second, and then threw his arms around her and pulled her into a tight embrace. He rested his right cheek on top of her head as he closed his eyes and continued to hold her in his arms. A tear rolled down his face as he held on to her. He pulled her away from him to look her over and make sure not a hair on her had been harmed. Then he pulled her back into his arms.

"Damn, Yaseer, you act like I just came back from the dead or something. It's ok, I'm ok," Paris spat in a quiet tone.

"I didn't know where you were, if you were ok, if you had been harmed. I didn't know. Please don't, don't do that again, P. Please don't do that again. I know you were mad at me for that bullshit I pulled, but on my life, I wouldn't be able to take another breath on this earth if I lost you, too."

Paris took in his words and realized this may not have been the best time to run off, but she couldn't help it. Time alone to herself away from everybody was the only time she could get all her cries out, think, and get her emotions together before dealing with a situation. However, the last time she did that, she ended up with a battered face and someone forcing themselves on her. She figured since London knew where she was, she was good. But then again, it was London who knew where she was the last time, and by the time Yaseer found out where she was, it was too late. Thinking about how she'd just run off, Paris understood her mistake. However, it was Yaseer that brought this about, as he had before. Loving him was dangerous because he had the ability to rip her soul to pieces, bit by bit, and he didn't even realize it.

"I'm sorry, Yaseer, but it's not like I didn't let someone know where I was. And to be quite honest, I would have never ran off had you not had your dick down some random bitch's throat. Answer me this, is this the first time you let that little *thot* bucket swallow you? Better yet, in all honesty, have you ever fucked the hoe? And please, I am begging you, please, don't lie to me because, on everything I love, I promise I will find out the truth," Paris questioned as she stepped away from Yaseer, crossed her arms over, her chest, and waited for an answer.

"Truthfully, no, this is not the first time she has gave me some dome. Ever since all that bullshit happened with Ezra and Ariel, on my life, I swear I had fell back hard on shawty and been on the straight and narrow with you. She just caught me at a moment when she knew I was vulnerable. I fucked up bad, ma. I will admit that. But no, I've never had sex with her. Never would," Yaseer answered.

"Hole up, so this bitch has been around for almost two years?" Paris questioned. All Yaseer could do was nod his head up and down. Before realizing what was about to happen, Paris' hand flew across Yaseer face, causing his head to turn with the slap.

"Two years, Yaseer, two fuckin' years this hoe been around? *Why?* Why is she still around? Why do you even still have her working in yo shit? That bitch should've been gone. That's why her dumb ass sat there like she was muhfuckin' King Kong when I told her punk ass to move! And I would have never known anything if I had not walked in on her with yo dick in her mouth, and you expect me to believe that you never fucked her. Man, fuck outta here," Paris spat as she mushed him in the head and walked past him with tears rolling down her face.

"Paris. Paris!" Yaseer called out once more.

She just wanted to shower and lay down for a few before she met up with London. She should have known better than anyone that Yaseer was not going to let her be great at all. It would be too much like right. She tried her best to walk as fast as she could to the bathroom so that she could shut the door, lock him out, and enjoy a nice long hot shower in peace. She had heard enough of his bullshit for one day. She had just made it over the threshold to the bathroom and was about to shut the door when Yaseer stuck his foot in the door to block her from closing it.

"Oh my God, would you please just leave me the fuck alone? Just leave me the fuck alone, man," Paris yelled as she walked over to the shower, turned it on, stripped out of the clothes that she had on, and stepped into the shower. Paris relished in the feeling of the steaming hot water that hit her caramel colored skin when she stepped in.

Paris leaned her head back in the shower and just enjoyed the warmth of the water. Yaseer had gotten very quiet. She hoped he'd left out of the bathroom and would just grant her the space that she needed so that she could think things through and decide rather or not she wanted to stay in this relationship. Paris felt the cool breeze of the shower being opened, and before she could react, she felt the warmth of Yaseer's hands around her waist as he pulled her to him and wrapped his arms around her.

As mad as she was at him, anytime he had her in his arms like that, it was hard to fight him, and at that moment, she didn't feel like fighting with him. She just wanted to relax and let the pain ease out through her pores. She leaned her head back on his chest and just took a moment to relax. She wasn't even mad at the fact that he had a bitch giving him head. It was the fact that he kept the chick around that she couldn't deal with. Paris inhaled deeply when she felt his warm lips on her neck. Her mind was saying move away, he doesn't deserve it, but her treacherous body, on the other hand, was being very defiant and downright disrespectful. It was literally craving his touch. Her kitty jumped as his massive had traveled down her abdomen past her scar to the apex between her legs. Paris moaned as she felt his fingers began to part her flower. She felt him slip two fingers inside of her womanly core and couldn't help but to let out a moan. Her hips began to move involuntarily to the feel of his touch. She placed her hand over his to try and move his hand, to no avail.

Keeping his fingers inside of her, Yaseer began stepping forward, causing her to step forward as well until she pressed against the shower wall. Yaseer placed his free hand beside her head on the shower wall as his other hand continued to play in her center. Paris' bottom lip slacked a little as he began to speed his fingers up. The faster his fingers went, the faster his her hips went. Yaseer bent down and sucked her bottom lip into his mouth before letting it go and sticking his tongue out to trace her lip. Then he sucked her lip back in his mouth and let it go again.

Paris was getting tired of playing she wanted him and she wanted him right now. She turned around in his embrace, wrapped her right leg around his waist, and pulled him to her. She used one hand to pull his head down to hers so that she could kiss him as she used her other hand to guide his wood into the entrance of her honey trap. She rubbed the tip up and down her moistness before placing it at her center, and then taking her hand, pulling his waist closer to her, making his member go further inside of her.

Yaseer inhaled deeply at the feeling of being inside her. Out of all the women he had been with, none of them ever made him feel the way Paris made him feel, especially when he was inside of her. Yaseer couldn't hold out any longer, he pushed all the way forward until he reached the hilt.

"Fuck," Yaseer muttered under his breath as he slowly began moving in and out of Paris. He couldn't help but to look down as his manhood went in and out of Paris' womanhood.

Paris dug her nails into his back as he continued to pump in and out of her. She couldn't help but bite her bottom lip as she too looked down at his dick going in and out of her tight wet pussy. The feeling of him inside of her, coupled with the hot water beating down on their bodies, was almost enough to send her over the edge. Paris' hips moved in sync with Yaseer's. Feeling she was close, Yaseer began to pump faster and faster. He couldn't help but to grip her ass as he continued to pump harder and harder.

"Uh, uh… Oh shiitt… Ya, Yaa, Yaseer, I'm bouta, I'm 'bout to cu, cuumm," Paris stuttered out.

"Um hmm, give me that shit. Let daddy get that, ma," Yaseer spat in a low voice in her ear.

Yaseer slowed down a little, took his fingers and began playing with her pearl as he slid in and out of her wet center.

"Oh shit. Oh shit," was all Paris could get out before she bit her bottom lip and squirted all on him.

"Wait, wait," Paris muttered as Yaseer continued to pump, causing her to cum again, which set off his own release. Feeling him releasing his warm seed inside of her, Paris pushed him back forcefully enough to dislodge him from her so that she could drop down to her knees and take him into her warm mouth. All Yaseer could do was gasp at the amazing feeling of her sucking his seeds out of him like a Hoover vacuum.

He palmed the back of her head as Paris continued sucking him off. She took the cum he had graciously filled her mouth with and spit it on his dick. Then she sucked it back off as she used her hand to pump. Yaseer felt like he was damn near having an out-of-body experience as he came once again. His face contorted a little as he looked down at Paris, who was looking up at him with her beautiful light brown slanted eyes as she swallowed his cum. Paris licked her lips, stood up and brought her lips next to his ear.

"This changes nothing. My apologies, lil daddy, you caught me at a moment you knew I was vulnerable," Paris spat in a sultry voice, walked around him, grabbed her Dove body wash, washed up, and got out of the shower, leaving Yaseer in the shower stuck in the same spot trying to figure out what just happened.

Chapter 19

Yaseer tried his hardest to quell his anger that was beginning to boil. He wasn't in the mood to be dealing with this relationship shit right now. In less than sixteen hours he was going to be saying goodbye to his baby sister forever. As much as it bothered him, he was going to give Paris the space both she and he needed before one of them ended up saying something that neither could take back, or ended up killing one another.

Yaseer finished washing up, got out of the shower, dried off, and then made his way into of their room. He grabbed some boxers, a black wife beater, and a pair of black footie socks out of his dresser drawer, then proceeded to his closet and grabbed a fresh black T, and a pair of black True Religion Jeans. He looked at Paris laying in the bed reading some book by a nigga named CA$H called *Thugs Cry 2*. Yaseer couldn't do nothing but shake his head at the title as he walked out of the room. That title was some real shit 'cause he swore in the last two years he had cried more times than he had ever cried in his lifetime.

Yaseer walked down to the guest room that he always slept in when he was in trouble, threw his clothes on, and then walked over to the closet to grab his spare shoulder holster. He put it on, then walked over to the nightstand beside the bed and grabbed his two Glock .26's, placed them in their proper spots on his holster, put on his crew's chain, slipped on his black timbs, and smoothed a hand over his head. He walked into the kids' rooms to check on them to see if they were still napping. He peeked in each of the boys' crib and saw that YJ was knocked out and that Jaseer was missing in action. His boys were like night and day. YJ was the night owl and Jaseer was the early bird. Yaseer pulled the covers up on YJ, then left the room. He walked down to his room to make sure Paris actually had Jaseer.

Once he saw that she did, he proceeded downstairs, grabbed his keys to his 2016 blacked out Charger, and headed out to see what mischief he could get into. He was really in the mood to send somebody to meet the Good Lord. It was time someone else felt his pain. With that in his mind, he got in the car and decided to go on a mission to check out his clubs, as well as his traps. The moment he spotted a fuck up, the person who caused it would be one of the first to go. As Yaseer drove off, he pulled out his phone and scrolled down to his dad's number. He had questions about his mom and there was only one person that could answer any questions he had about her, his pops.

"What's good, son," Eric spat into Yaseer's ear.

"None much, pops. How you doing? They still treating you good up there?" Yaseer questioned as he connected his phone to the Bluetooth in the car and placed his phone down in the console.

"Yeah, they been treating yo ole man like a king in here. Anything I want, I get, except for my freedom, ya feel me."

"Yeah, I feel you on that pops."

"How y'all holding up? Y'all all set for tomorrow?"

"Yeah, we are. You asking me how we holding up, how are *you* holding up?"

"As best as I can for a person in this situation. I hate that I can't be there to see my baby girl one last time, but it is what it is. I made my bed so now I gotta lay in it. Just make sure y'all send my baby off right, a'ight."

"Of course, pops, nothing but the best for Brooklyn."

"How you adjusting to Erin?"

"I'm not, and not because I don't want to, it's just hard to do so at the moment. It's hard as fuck to look at her. It's a constant reminder that the baby sister I grew up with and helped raise when y'all went away is gone and never coming back," Yaseer answered, choking up a little just thinking of her. Deciding he needed to change the conversation for both his and his dad's benefit, he decided to ask about the one person he called about, his mom. He didn't know why, but something didn't sit right with him about her.

"Yo, listen, did you know moms was out?"

"She what? Come again."

"She's out of prison, pops," Yaseer replied.

"Son of a bitch. Aye, son, let me call you back."

"Aye, pops, before you go, can you please just tell me one thing? I hate to even ask this because she's my mom, but something in my gut is not sitting right about her. Is she trustworthy?"

"I won't speak ill to you about yo moms, but before I go, I will let you in on this because I feel like you're old enough to hear it. To make a long story short, it wasn't my right hand's doing that put us here, or better yet where I'm at, as you were led to believe. NeNe and CA$H said it the best, *Trust No Bitch*. Oh, and one mo thing, keep her away from anything and anyone you love or they'll be gone, too. Love left that woman's heart a long time ago. She is as cold-hearted as they come, and for reasons I don't care to elaborate on at the moment, she is hell bent on hurting and destroying any and every one close to me," Eric replied as he hung up the phone.

Chapter 20

Yaseer hung up the phone more confused and conflicted than before he called his dad, and the look on his face showed it. Deep, deep down in his gut, he had a feeling that some crazy shit was about to pop off that would change the course of his life forever. Yaseer made a few more phone calls before reaching his first destination, Day 1. Yaseer got out of his car and walked inside of his strip club, ready to take his anger out on the one person that played a part in the bullshit that had Paris on one. Yaseer walked to the dressing room, where he knew she would be chilling at since it wasn't time for her to go on stage yet. Yaseer pushed the door open, and just as he thought, she was sitting in there yapping her mouth to this mixed stripper named Becky.

"Scuse me, baby girl, lemme holla at Sasha right quick," Yaseer requested in a cool tone.

"Come on, shawty, I ain't got all day to be foolin' around wit cho ass," Yaseer spat at Sasha as he turned and began walking out of the dressing room. Yaseer walked to his office, ready to give shawty the business. He opened the door and stepped aside for her enter. Once she was all the way in his office, he shut the door and locked it.

"You might as well not even sit down, shawty," Yaseer spat as he walked over to the chair behind his desk and sat down. Yaseer reached in his top drawer and grabbed the remote to his Bluetooth stereo, pressed the power button, connected his phone to it, and put on Pandora. Yaseer smiled to himself as he heard the beat to Future's song *Monster* come on. It literally fit the moment for him.

"Strip," he commanded as he began to turn the music up, not wanting anyone to hear what was about to go down.

"Anything for you, Papi, I knew you'd be back for more," Sasha replied as she began to strip and twerk her ass to the beat of the song.

Yaseer bobbed his head as he listened to one of his favorite songs. He lit a blunt, leaned back in his chair, and watched her dance. He looked over her well-toned cinnamon colored body. Yaseer couldn't lie, shawty was bad, but she had some real shit to learn. Sasha flipped her long jet black curls over her shoulder as she turned around, giving Yaseer a full view of her enhanced ass that every female in America thought a nigga wanted. Yaseer looked at the butterfly wings she had tattooed on each ass cheek. Putting his blunt in the ashtray, he got up and walked up behind Sasha as she continued to shake her ass for him. Yaseer stood right behind her. While she twerked, he smacked her ass, making her more excited. He couldn't help but shake his head. She wasn't even aware of the work he was really 'bout to put in.

"Damn, I'ma miss seeing this ass," Yaseer mumbled under his breath. In one swift move he grabbed a fist full of her hair and yanked her head back to him and placed his mouth near her ear. "You thought that shit was cute earlier, huh? You see my wife come in and thought it was real cute to sit there after she had just caught you with my dick down your throat, huh?" Yaseer questioned through gritted teeth as he tightened the grip he had on her hair.

"She, she was smiling. I thought she was cool with it until she pulled her piece. I'm so, so sorry. I didn't mean to disrespect you, Papi. It won't happen again," she replied in a voice full of fear, causing her Dominican accent to come out thick.

"You damn right it won't," Yaseer spat as he quickly pulled his piece and decorated his clothes and office with her brains. Yaseer finally let go of the grip he had on her head, stepped back, and watched as her lifeless body collapsed on the huge rug he had placed there earlier that day after Paris had left, knowing he was going to splatter shawty's shit on it later for the stunt that she pulled. Yaseer took his shirt off as he walked to his bathroom to shower and change clothes. Once he was all cleaned up, Yaseer called his cleaning crew to tell them he had a body that needed to be disposed of. Yaseer sat down on the bed that he had in his office and relit the blunt that he had put out earlier. He laid back and waited for the crew to come and dispose of the body. Hearing the code knock on his office door, he got up and opened it.

"Sup, Drew. Sup, Duke," Yaseer greeted as he opened his door wide enough to let them in.

"Got damn, nigga, shawty must've really pissed you off," Duke said as he walked further into the office.

"Um hm," Yaseer answered as he shut his door and locked it.

"Y'all know how to handle that. Take the bitch to the chop shop. I'll have Zyon come back later get the tapes. Make sure y'all lock up," Yaseer said as he collected his belongings and left.

Chapter 21

Yaseer exhaled as he sat in the driver's seat of his whip with his head resting on his headrest. Then he cranked up the car and proceeded to his next destination, to check his traps.

One by one, he rode by his traps and was getting slightly aggravated that out of all days, no one wanted to fuck up today. Everyone was on point today. Yaseer was about ready to put a hot one in anyone right about now. His thirst for blood had yet to be fulfilled by that one killing he'd just done. He wanted everyone to feel his pain, and come hell or high water, somebody was about to really catch it, and catch it bad, Yaseer thought to himself as he pulled up to his last trap on South Blvd.

He had a trap house just about everywhere in Charlotte and his trap house on the white folks' side of town was booming. Believe it or not, white people got more geeked than black folk, they just knew how to hide their addictions when they needed to. Majority of the time, only their lover, the drug dealer, and the good Lord ever really knew that they were addicted to anything. Yaseer checked his clip to make sure it was fully loaded, just in case anybody wanted to jump bad. Then he opened the hidden compartment he had on the floor on the passenger side of his car and pulled out an army knife that he took from some old cat that owed him money a few days ago. Yaseer pressed the lock button on his key ring and walked up the steps to the beautiful home that he kept filled with dope. Yaseer knocked on the door without using the secret code knock to see if an idiot would be dumb enough to open the door. Nobody came.

"Damn," Yaseer muttered as he pulled out his keys to open the door.

Oh, somebody was about to get this work. One little fuck up and somebody was taking a one way trip to meet their maker. Yaseer walked through the house, seeing nothing but everyone doing what he paid them to do, working. He was almost done checking everything when he saw a cat named EZ grab some bands off the table to go put in the safe in the storage room where they kept the money until it was time for it to get picked up by Liam. Yaseer watched as dude unknowingly dropped a band on the floor as he walked to his destination. Yaseer's heart almost jumped for joy and he couldn't help the evil smile that started to spread across his face as he realized he had found his second victim for today.

"Aye, bruh, you dropped some," Yaseer said as he walked up and picked up that stack that had dropped on the floor and handed it to him.

"Matter fact, let me take some of that from you. You seem like you got your hands full," Yaseer said in a voice filled with a little too much excitement.

EZ looked at Yaseer as if he had grown two heads. In the past five years that he'd worked for Yaseer, he had never seen him that happy, and he meant never. He didn't know rather to be alarmed or not, so he just went with the flow of things and handed some of the money to Yaseer.

"Thanks, boss man," EZ replied, then kept walking to the storage room. He just wanted to put the money in the safe so that he could get out of there and go home to his wife and baby girl. It was movie night and he didn't want to be late. Once the money was in the safe, they both turned to leave the room.

"Aye, man, I wanna say thank you for making sure my bank was straight," Yaseer said as he held his right hand out to shake up with EZ. As soon as EZ slapped hands with Yaseer, he pulled him into a manly hug and let his blade pierce the flesh of EZ's abdomen. Yaseer pulled the knife out and plunged it back in again and again, making sure to pull upwards and twist it the last time he sent it into EZ's gut. Yaseer patted him on the back with the knife still in his hand.

"Gots to be more careful," Yaseer spat as he let EZ's body crumble to the ground. Before he could get all the way out of the door, he heard EZ trying to say a word. Yaseer walk over to him and squatted down so that he could try and see if he could understand what he was saying.

"Da, Da, Mya," he coughed out before he took his last breath. Yaseer frowned his face up. "Damya," Yaseer said under his breath as he made a mental to note to find out who she was.

***

Two hours and another change of clothes later, Yaseer pulled up at Kai'yan's house, which was where they had decided to have Brooklyn's wake. Yaseer pulled out his phone, went to his gallery, pressed the camera, and clicked on the last picture he took in his phone. It was the last picture him and Brooklyn ever took together. They were standing in his living room. Brooklyn was pointing down to her belly with both of her index fingers with her head tilted smiling, and Yaseer was squatted down pointing to her protruding belly, making a silly face. It was their thing. Just about every time they took a picture together, one of them had to goof off in the picture. Now taking a picture with anyone else would never feel the same. A lone tear escaped Yaseer's eye as he put his phone away and stepped out of the car.

Yaseer walked the short distance to the door and rang the doorbell. He put his hands in his pocket as he waited on someone to the answer the door. From the looks of it, he was the last one to arrive. Even Paris's car was already there.

Yaseer didn't have to wait long before someone came to the door.

"Hey," London spat dryly as she opened the door for Yaseer to come in. She was still pissed at him for what he had done to her sister and for putting his hands on her.

"Sup, L," Yaseer responded as he put his head down and walked past her into the house. He couldn't even bring himself to look at her. He knew he fucked up bad with London because for once since she had known him, she had nothing smart to say to him when she opened the door. Normally, when he showed up late, she always had something smart to say, but not today. Yaseer knew he needed to apologize, he just couldn't bring himself to do it at the moment. He had done enough apologizing for one day. Right now, he just wanted to chill with the people that he loved and reminisce on his baby sister's life.

"Sup, bruh," Yaseer said as he walked into the living room.

"Sup, Seer," Kai'yan said as he got up to greet him. Neither one of them had seen one another since Brooklyn had died. Actually, Kai'yan had kept his distance from everyone except his baby girl because being around them was a constant reminder that Brooklyn was gone and he definitely was trying his best to avoid being around Erin. It was just too much. He knew eventually he would get to the point where he could hang around her like he did the rest of the crew, but he didn't think he could do it any longer than he had to between then and tomorrow.

"How you holding up, bruh?" Yaseer asked.

"I'm hanging in there as best as I can, bruh. How 'bout you?"

"Same here, fam. Where's lil momma?"

"In her room being spoiled by Liam's ass."

"Well he might as well get ready to fall back 'cause big unk here now," Yaseer replied as he walked up the three stairs, out of the den, through the kitchen, then made a right in the living room that led to the hallway where her bedroom was located. Yaseer stopped at the door that read Missy. Kai'yan had decided to name her that instead of the name that he and Brooklyn had picked out together because when she was pregnant and Missy would be kicking a lot, balling up, or getting under her rib cage, she would gently tap her belly and say, "All right now, Ms. Missy." Yaseer took a deep breath, then opened the door to her room. It was time for him to start building a bond with his niece.

"Sup, lil bruh," Yaseer greeted in a quiet tone as he stepped into the room and shut the door behind him.

"Sup." Liam responded coolly. Yup, Liam was still pissed at him, too. Liam checked himself before he got up and passed Missy to Yaseer. He could feel himself getting upset just by looking at Yaseer and he didn't wanna pass that negative energy down to Missy.

He knew he needed to get himself together so that he could deal with Yaseer these next few days because it's what Brooklyn would want. She wouldn't want them mad at each other and cutting up at her funeral. In fact, she always said that when she passed away she wanted everyone to turn up at her repast and really celebrate the time she was allotted to have breath. Liam stopped in his tracks at the thought of his sister.

"Look, bruh, I know you going through some shit. But in the midst of going through it, remember we lost her too and you're not the only one going through some shit. I forgive you for putting your hands on my wifey. Just don't let the shit happen again. I'm here when you're ready to talk," Liam spat as he walked out of the room.

A tear slipped out of Yaseer's eye as he sat down in the rocking chair with Missy. He leaned back with the infant cradled in the crook of his arm and began to slowly rock back and forth with her in his arm as he looked down at her. More tears began to fall down his face as he continued to look down at his beautiful niece. She had just the right amount of both Brooklyn and Kai'yan. She was so tiny compared to the boys.

"Hhheeeyy, Miss Missy," Yaseer said just above a whisper as he continued to rock.

"If your mom could see you now, she would be head over heels in love with you," Yaseer whispered in a quiet voice as he swayed back in forth in the rocking chair. Yaseer rocked Missy for a few more minutes before putting the sleeping baby in her bassinet, tucking her in, and leaving out of the room.

Yaseer went back to the den, where everyone had seemed to migrate, found a seat, and sat down. It felt a little awkward because just about everyone in the room was upset with him for one reason or another, except Kai'yan and Zyon. Paris watched as Yaseer pulled out his phone and started to play on it. She could tell he was feeling a little uneasy, and although she was still upset with him, she would not let him feel like he was alone these next few days. She loved him too much for that. She exhaled a deep breath before turning her attention towards Erin.

"Hey, sweetie, do you mind holding Chaunte for me?" Paris asked before placing the toddler, who was infatuated with the game on her Nabi, on Erin's lap. Then she got up and made her way over to Yaseer. She was going to try her best to push the problems they were having to the back of her mind. It was going to be a difficult task, but she knew that she could do it.

"Mind if I sit beside you?" Paris asked when she was almost to him.

"Naw, ion mind," Yaseer replied as he scooted over on the huge love seat to make room for her to sit down. For a moment, they were quiet as they listened to their friends and family talk about Brooklyn, not saying a word to anyone or each other.

"I miss her so much, P. Damn, I miss her," Yaseer said in a low voice, loud enough for only Paris to hear him.

"I know, bae, I miss her, too," Paris replied.

"It just feels so unreal. Like I can't believe that she's gone. Why'd God have to take her, P? Why'd he have to take her? I know that we not supposed to question him, but, but why her? He could have took me. I would have gone willingly in her place. I would have went, P," Yaseer spat as tears began to run down his face. He just wanted this whole nightmare to be over with.

"Ssshh, sshh, I know it's hard right now, but it'll get easier, love," Paris responded as she pulled Yaseer's head down to her chest.

One by one, everyone from the crew came and stood by Yaseer to help comfort him as he laid on Paris, bawling his eyes out. Everyone felt his pain because it was pretty much the same pain they had in their hearts, especially Kai'yan.

Feeling himself getting overwhelmed with emotion, Kai'yan decided to walk outside on his back porch, making sure to stop in the kitchen to grab himself a beer. Stepping outside, he flung his dreads back so that they were out of his face and sat down in the wooden chair he had placed out there. Kai'yan sipped on his Corona as he looked out over the pond that was in his backyard. So many memories of Brooklyn flooded his mind, and for a moment, he started to feel a little depressed, knowing that she would miss their beautiful baby girl growing up. Kai'yan laid his head back on the chair and closed his eyes. Hearing the sliding door open, he slowly opened his eyes to see who it was.

"You good, fam?" London asked as she stepped onto the patio, followed by Liam.

"Naw, not really, but I'm sure I will be over time," he replied with Liam nodding his head in agreement. One by one, everyone migrated outside with a drink of their own. For hours on hours, they sat talking about Brooklyn and speaking about the memories they each had of her. They decided to forgo having her body present at the house like most wakes, and instead decided they would all say goodbye to her one last time, tomorrow, at the service.

Chapter 22

It had been a whole month since Brooklyn had been buried and everyone was starting to finally adjust to the idea of her being gone. For the first time in a long time, the crew didn't have anyone coming at them sideways. It was kind of weird for them because for almost two years it seemed like every day was a fight. But everyone knew that it was almost always a calm before the storm.

"A, yo, Easy E," London called as she walked into Erin's new apartment using the key that Erin had given her.

"Sup, L."

"What cho ass in here burning up, gul," London cracked while walking down the hallway to the kitchen.

"Deez nutz," Erin responded with a smile on her face as London came into view.

"Oh shit, lemme find out baby can burn," London spat as she looked at the lemon pepper wings, collard greens, and mashed potatoes with gravy that was cooking on the stove.

"Is that what I think it is?" London questioned as she sniffed the air. "Is that mac and cheese that I smell?" London asked as she pushed Erin out of the way with her hips and opened up the oven to take a peek.

"Yaaasss, God, yyyaaasss," London exclaimed, then caught a slight attitude.

"Why yo punk ass ain't never cook when you lived with me? I just assumed you couldn't cook."

"I honestly don't know why I didn't. It was kinda weird living with you all at first, then it just became a habit of me either ordering food or you cooking."

"Umm hmm. I guess I'll accept that excuse," London said with a shrug of her shoulders as she grabbed a clean spoon out of the dish rack, got a spoon full of the greens, blew them, and put them in her mouth, sucking air into her mouth as she at them, trying to keep the hot vegetables from burning her tongue.

"Oh my Gaawwwddd. Will you be my baby momma?" London asked as she got on one knee. Erin couldn't help but to laugh at London's shenanigans.

"Girl them greens is good as fuck," London said as she smacked her lips together and stood back up to her full height.

"Well thank ya, dahling, and no, I will not accept your offer to be your baby momma. Liam is not about to kick my ass over you. I swear, that nigga becomes a whole live fool when it comes to anything that concerns London Danyella Smith."

"I won't tell if you won't," London replied.

"Tell what?" Liam said as he walked into Erin's apartment, followed by Yaseer, Kai'yan, and Zyon.

"Nun yo business, ole nosey ass," London spat.

"Who you spittin' that hot shit to, shawty?" Liam asked as he walked up behind London.

"Uuumm, the man down the street and around the corner," she replied.

"Yeah, a'ight, dats who yo shawt ass betta be talkin' to," Liam replied as he pushed up on London.

"Eeww, would you two take that lovey dovey shit outta my damn kitchen? Don't nobody wanna see that."

"That's what I'm saying, though," Zyon chimed in with "amen" coming from both Kai'yan and Yaseer.

"Man, fuck y'all wit y'all ole hatin' asses. Y'all just mad cause y'all ain't getting' none. Come on, bae," London responded as she grabbed Liam's hand and pulled him with her out of the kitchen.

"Damn," Liam muttered under his breath as he walked behind her, looking at how fat her booty had gotten since they had been together. The black spandex shorts that she had on cupped the bottom of her ass cheeks, making her butt look even bigger. Yaseer shook his head as he watched the two love sick birds walk out of the kitchen.

"Five bucks says she'll get pregnant tonight," Kai'yan betted.

"Twenty says she already pregnant," Yaseer wagered.

"I'll second that," Zyon said.

"Thirty says y'all all wrong wit y'all nasty asses," Erin spat as she turned the stove off.

"Says the person in here that don't have kids," Yaseer cracked as he came to peek into the pots as well.

"Man, if y'all don't get y'all greedy asses out my kitchen."

"Got damn, you stay kickin' niggas out the damn kitchen, won't never let nobody be great," Yaseer spat as they all turned around to leave the kitchen.

In a weird way, it kinda became comforting that Erin was around. It was like Brooklyn was still there, even though she wasn't. Yaseer liked to joke that maybe God just decided to give Brooklyn a new body.

"Nope, I sure won't," Erin responded as she followed them out of kitchen, only to turn back around to go fix their plates.

"Oh shit na, she cook and she serves," Zyon cracked.

"I'm in a good mood today. I just got hired on at the job I applied for when I first moved down here," Erin replied as she put both Zyon's and Yaseer's plates in front of them.

"And what job is that?" Yaseer questioned with a frown on his face.

"A job down at Presbyterian Hospital as a surgical assistant."

"How come I didn't know you had a degree in that?"

"Maybe 'cause you never bothered to even as me about rather or not I went to college."

"Well I'll be damn. Congratulations, lil sis. When do you start?"

"On Monday, and I can't wait," Erin stated with excitement in her voice.

"What's all the ruckus about?" Liam asked as he walked back into the kitchen.

"E got a job down at Presbyterian. Aye, did you know shawty is a certified surgical assistant?" Zyon questioned.

"Yup!"

"Da hell, how yo ass knew and we didn't?" Yaseer questioned.

"Maybe because I'm that nigga and actually was curious if she went to college or not. Have you not seen her with her glasses on? She look like a geek," Liam cracked as he dodged a hit from Erin, who stuck her tongue out at him.

"What else don't I know?" Yaseer questioned as he took a sip of the sprite that Erin had just given him.

"That I'm a transgender," Erin answered, causing Yaseer to spit his drink out. Erin burst out laughing. She just wanted to fuck with him for that wisecrack he made earlier about her not having any kids.

"Bet yo ass a learn not to fuck with me no more Mr. *we can tell who don't have no kids.*"

"I oughta beat yo lil ass," Yaseer said with a smile on his face as he grabbed a napkin and cleaned himself up.

"Yea, yea. Sssooo what's on the agenda today?" Erin asked.

"Well, nothing much that I can think of, besides the usual. Oh, and my moms supposed to be stopping by my crib later on," Yaseer answered. "What y'all got planned?" he questioned.

"Shit," Zyon replied.

"Same here," Kai'yan responded.

"What about you Liam?"

"Nun at the moment, unless L decides she wants to do something," Liam said as he took a bite of the chicken. "Good lawd, gul, these lemon pepper wings on point. You sure you wanna have your own spot? You can always have your old room back," Liam said as he took another bite of the chicken wing. Erin shook her head as she laughed at Liam. He and London were definitely two of a kind.

"Why thank you, sir! And yup, I'm more than sure I want my own space, especially after living with you and London's freaky deeky asses. I think y'all done had enough sex for everyone in both North and South Carolina." Liam almost choked on his chicken.

"You know what? Yup, keep yo ass over here. I'll just come over here for dinner," Liam replied.

"Nuh ugh, ion know who you think gonna be cooking it. London's cooking is just as good."

"But she be starving me, though, sis. I swea fo M&M's she tyrna kill me. Look how skinny I done got since you met me. She only feed me three times a day."

"Nigga, that's all the hell yo ass need. How many meals yo ass think you supposed to have?" Yaseer chimed in.

"As many as I want, nigga," Liam spat as he grabbed a chair at the table and continued to eat his food.

"Where London go?" Erin asked.

"In your room knocked the fuck out."

"Run me my money," Yaseer spat. Both Kai'yan and Erin pulled out the money they'd bet Yaseer and paid him, knowing that they had already lost. Ever since Brooklyn had passed, London was either found stuffing her face or sleeping. Erin was hoping that today would be different, but nope, it would have been too much like right.

"Aaww hell, what the hell ya done bet this fool on now?" Liam asked. Everybody just looked around before focusing their attention on their plates in front of them. "Oh, so now y'all asses can't talk."

"Hmm hmm," Erin cleared her throat. A certain someone at this table, I won't say no names, started a lil wager that London was pregnant," Erin commented as she turned her head and looked directly at Yaseer.

"Yo ass stay hustlin' folk out they money," Liam spat as he shook his head with a smile on his face.

"Y'all know his fertile ass can smell a fertile female ten yards away," Liam spat with a smile on his face. "Anywho, have you talked to dad again since the last time?" Liam asked, successfully changing the subject.

"Nah, I haven't heard from him since he found out that moms was out. You?" Yaseer shot back.

"Um um," Liam replied as he shook his head.

"Do you really think that mom had something to do with them getting locked up?" Zyon asked in a quiet voice.

"Honestly, I believe if she did, it was her plan for only dad to go, but she ended up getting screwed over as well. What I do know for sure is that something ain't right with this whole situation, and I keep getting this uneasy feeling that some crazy shit 'bout to pop off. I can't explain it. I just got this feeling, bruh," Yaseer responded.

"I thought I was the only one who was having that feeling, fam," Liam said as he stood up from his leaning position on the counter.

"I got Cakez and Juelz looking into some shit for me. If they come back with the info that I think they gone come back with, then we 'bout to have a rude awakening. I will truly believe that everything that we have been through these past few years was due to the sins of our father," Yaseer said as he leaned back in his chair.

Royal Nicole

Chapter 23

Two hours later, Yaseer was finally on his way back home. He had been out all day making sure all of his businesses were on point and trying to get things set into place just in case he had to go to war with one of the people he truly loved with all his heart. But one thing Yaseer had learned over the past few years was the ones who you loved the most and who claimed that they loved you were the ones who often betrayed you the most.

Yaseer pulled his car into his garage, let the garage door down, got out, and went in the house. Yaseer walked through the house, checking it to make sure that everything was in place and that no one was in the house. Then he walked into his room and flopped down on his back in his bed. It didn't seem the same with Paris not living with him anymore. A week after Brooklyn had been buried, Paris decided it was best if she moved out and got her own place. She even decided to take the girls with her so he wouldn't have to worry about who would keep them when he had to handle business. Plus, she felt as though they were just as much her daughters as they were his because she had been the one taking care of them ever since Zyon sent Ariel to meet her maker. So in her head, she was their mom. When they got older, they would only have memories of her helping to raise them, not their birth mother. And on top of that, she wanted them to build a bond with the boys from an early age.

Yaseer closed his eyes and put his arm over his eyes, trying to figure out where everything went wrong with them. He swore to himself if he ever got her back that he was going to do right by her. And he was more than determined to get her back, especially since he had been hearing about this nigga named Seven coming around. He didn't know who he was or where he came from, but he'd better hope that he never ran into him at Paris' house, or anywhere else, because if he did, it might just be the last time that he ran into anything. Yaseer was ready to bust his head to the white meat and he didn't even know him, but he did know he didn't want him around Paris, thinking he had a shot at anything with her. Rather she knew it or not, she was still his and always would be. He wasn't ready to let go of her just yet. He only stepped back to let her do her thing until she was ready to come home. Yaseer sat up, deciding that he needed to see her, even if she didn't want to see him.

***

"Oh my God, Sev, you and your damn road rage. I'ma need you to get that under control," Paris spat into the speaker of her phone as she sat on the couch flipping the TV channels and eating a Heath toffee milkshake from the cookout earlier that day. She had just finished cleaning little odds and ins throughout her house when Seven hit her line. It felt good to deal and talk with someone who wasn't in *that* life. It was refreshing to for once in her life just live without the worries that came along with being Yaseer's girl. At times, she missed him and what they had. But she just couldn't do it anymore, at least not at the moment. She wasn't quite ready for round three with him just yet.

Paris put her milkshake on the coffee table, put her feet up on the couch, and laid back. The TV was on low and she could hear the summer rain beating down her oversized living room windows. She had just gotten comfortable when she heard the doorbell to her humble abode ring.

"Who the hell?" Paris said under her breath as she sat up. "Hold on, Sev, let me see who at my door."

"Ok, and make sure you got that ratchet with you before you answer that door, shawty," Seven advised.

"Already in my hand, bae," Paris said as she put the phone down on the table and walked to the door to see who was ringing her doorbell so late at night without even so much as calling to let her know that they were on the way to her house.

Paris peeped out the peephole. With a look of confusion over her face, she unlocked and opened the door.

"Da hell, why yo goofy ass ain't tell me you was on the way over?"

"And spoil the look that's on your face now and not see you in them booty shorts?" Seven spat as he stepped through the threshold of Paris' house. Paris couldn't do anything but smile. The sight of him made her heart happy. She was glad he popped up on her.

Paris looked left and right outside before she shut the door. Then she followed Seven to her petite living room. Since she had moved out of the house that she and Yaseer shared, Seven had been by several times. She didn't know where their relationship would go, but what she did know was that   she was comfortable with where it was now. She wasn't quite ready to be in a relationship just yet, but the more Seven came over, the closer she got to being there.

"I thought yo black ass was on the way to the beach."

"I was, bbbuuuttt my heart wasn't in it because a certain someone wasn't going to be there," Seven said as he pulled Paris closer to him.

"Is that right?" Paris questioned as she rested her small hands on his chest.

"Um hm," Seven responded as he brought his lips down to Paris's.

Paris closed her eyes as his lips met hers and she couldn't help but let a little moan escape through her lips as his hands moved down to grab a handful of her ass. Paris wrapped her arms around his neck and began walking forward until Seven's legs hit the back of the sofa.

Seven broke the kiss for a minute as he sat down on the couch. Seven's heart skipped a beat as he looked up into her eyes and she began to straddle him.

Paris brought her lips back to his and began to slowly wind her hips on his lap as Seven held on tightly to her hips. Paris' heart began to speed up a little as she felt his hand moving upwards to the hem of her shirt. Paris broke the kiss and leaned back so that she could help him take her shirt off. Paris tossed her shirt aside. Then she used her hands to help Seven get out of his shirt faster and disposed of his shirt just like she had done hers. Paris brought her lips back to his in a haste. She moaned as Seven's tongue began to lightly trace her collar bone. She wrapped her arms around his neck and leaned her head back as she enjoyed the feeling of Seven's lips kissing a path down to her twin peaks. Paris gasped at the feeling of Seven sucking her nipple into his mouth. The feeling caused her to grind a little harder.

Seven brought his massive hand in between their bodies, slid his hand up her thigh, and pushed the spandex material of her shorts to the side. Her kitty jumped at the feeling of his finger sliding up and down the slit of her overly saturated pussy.

Paris bit her bottom lip as she looked into his eyes and he looked into hers. Paris let out a small moan as she felt him stick two fingers inside her dripping wet center. She brought her lips back to his. As he continued to finger fuck her, she began to wind her hips faster as she felt his pace pick up. For a moment, she thought she was having an out-of-body experience when he began to play with her womanly pearl as he continued to slide his fingers in and out of her slippery wet core. Just as he was about to lay her back on her back, they were both disturbed by a knock on the door. Paris slowly pulled away from Seven, and looked him deeply in the eyes. Her thoughts of him were put to a halt at the sound of someone knocking on her door again.

"I'll be right back," Paris said in a quiet voice as she pecked him on the lips, threw her shirt back on, and then went to see who in the hell was knocking on her door at that time of night. She knew it wasn't London because she had already spoken to her and London had told her that she and Liam had decided to go out of town at the spur of the moment. The closer Paris got to her front door, the more her stomach started to ball up with nerves.

"Please, God, don't let this be who I think it is," Paris prayed quietly. She was not in the mood to deal with bull tonight, but out of everyone, she only knew of one person who would show up at her house with no warning.

"Why are you at my house at this time of night, Yaseer?" Paris questioned as she flung the door open.

"Well hello to you, too. And damn I gotta have a reason to stop by now?"

"According to my watch, it's booty call time, so yup, you for damn sure better have a legit reason for coming over my house at this time of night other than tryna get your dick wet."

"I just wanted to check on you and my seeds, P. You hardly come by, and when you do, it's to drop the kids off or pick them up. Ion know how much longer I can do this. I miss my babies being at home with me. I miss you being home with me. I get it, P, I do. I know you need your space, and I'm tryna give you that, but damn, I swear I'm at the end of my ropes with this shit right here," Yaseer spat as he ran a massive hand over his face and inhaled then exhaled deeply. He could deal with a lot, but not this living situation. It was taking the life out of him. Paris and his kids where his rocks. Without them, he felt all he had to lean on was a pebble, and for a man like him in his position, that was very dangerous.

"Well who the fuck fault is it that you're at the end of your ropes, Yaseer? Whose fucking fault is it?"

"P, calm down, ma. I ain't even come over here to argue. To be honest, I just needed to see yo-" Yaseer was saying until his eyes spotted what he thought was another nigga in his girl's house.

"Aye, yo, you good, Pare?" Seven asked as he walked up behind her to see what was going on after hearing her raise her voice.

"Yeah, nigga, she good. Who da fuck is this nigga, P?"

"Oh naw, homie, you can direct that question right at me, and I will tell you who the fuck I am," Seven replied, feeling himself getting more heated by the moment.

"Dude, was I even talkin' to yo punk ass?" Yaseer spat.

"Ion give a fuck if you was or not. What you not 'bout to do is come over here raisin' on my shawty."

"Yo what? Nigga, how the fuck she gone be yo shawty when she already my wife? I advise you to get yo shit and get the fuck on through, lil partna," Yaseer responded, taking a step forward, calming just a little at the feel of Paris's small hands on his chest. Paris could feel Yaseer's heart racing. She knew if she didn't get a handle on him soon, Seven was going to be a dead man. Sure, Seven was a monster when he wanted or needed to be, but Yaseer, on the other hand, was a *beast,* and he owned that shit with pride. The fools who were brave enough to even try to jump bad at Yaseer normally ended up vanishing off the face of the earth like they never existed.

"*Yaseer,*" Paris called out to no avail.

"Wife? Naw, my dude, you and your delusional ass are the ones who need to leave," Seven replied.

"Yes, *my* wife. Now I'ma give you one last chance to get the fuck out before I bust yo whole shit all over these walls," Yaseer said in a deadly tone through gritted teeth.

Seven backed up, walked into the living room, and grabbed his piece, ready for whatever. He wasn't about to let not one nigga bitch him down. He didn't care who they were. As soon as Seven came around the corner to walk back to the front door, he saw the business end of Yaseer's glock, silencer intact, aiming at his head.

"Do you really wanna go there tonight, fam? You're very lucky that you're still alive and that's only because I'm not tryna piss my lady off no more than she already is by splattering yo shit all in her residence, especially with our kids here. But you really testing yo luck. Last warning, go on and get on through if you wanna live to see tomorrow," Yaseer spat as he gripped the handle of his tool tighter. Every fiber in his being was pleading with him to bust one off in dude's dome, but he was trying his hardest to be good for the sake of Paris and his babies.

"Nigga, who the fu-" Seven got out before Paris cut him off.

"Sev, just go 'cause this looney toon fool will literally shoot you and it won't be nothing that I could say or do to stop him once he gets that far."

"For real, Paris, you sending me away cause of this nig-ga?"

"Yes, I care too much about your safety to put you in harm's way any further. I'll talk to you later," Paris replied in a quiet tone as she opened her front door wider to allow Seven to pass by. As soon as Paris opened her door wider, she saw a car creeping by without any lights on.

"Seer, get in here now," Paris screamed, pulling him by the arm forcefully into the house.

As soon as Paris slammed the door shut and ducked down on the floor, she heard the sound of gunshots ringing out into her house. Yaseer put his body over Paris's to try and protect her from any gunshots or sharp objects that could harm her. Yaseer's heart rate sped erratically at the thought of anything happening to Paris. He didn't give two shits about himself when it came to her, and he vowed on everything that he loved he was going to find whatever idiot was brave enough to even come near Paris. He had just gotten a handle of the beast within him that craved the taste of blood when Brooklyn had died. And whoever had gotten big enough balls to try and kill his heart didn't know that they had just awakened that beast again, and its hunger was ten times worse.

Yaseer held onto his gun tight as he hovered over Paris. He was waiting patiently for everything to calm down so that he could rush outside to get the license plate to track the owner of the vehicle down. Hearing the shooting had stopped, Yaseer stood up, ready to push someone's wig back. Yaseer extended his hand to help Paris up when he heard her scream like someone had murdered her. Yaseer turned his head and looked in the direction that Paris was looking in. Yaseer shook his head and ran a hand over his face as he walked over to Seven.

"Damn," he muttered as he squatted down to check Seven's pulse.

"Calm down, P, he still has a pulse, but we gotta get him to the hospital ASAP," Yaseer said as he picked up Seven's limp body, tossed him over his shoulder, and carried him to the car, looking left and right over his shoulder to make sure that the coast was clear, followed by Paris.

"Aye, call Liam and tell him I need him and London back ASAP. Hit up the rest of the crew and tell them to meet us at the warehouse."

"Already on it," Paris spat as she got settled in the passenger seat. She looked over her shoulder at an unconscious Seven and couldn't help but to shed a tear. All she could think was that if it wasn't for her, he would've never been in this predicament. He didn't deserve this. He had too much going for himself and she vowed that if he survived this, then she would cut all ties with him for the sake of his safety. Paris swiped a runaway tear away from her face as she turned her head back to look out the window as Yaseer drove at top speed to the hospital. As mad as she was with Yaseer, she was more than grateful to him for trying his best get Seven to the hospital to save his life. It meant more to her than he would ever know.

Less than ten minutes later, they were pulling up to Huntersville Presbyterian. Paris jumped out of the car, and ran inside the hospital to get staff to come out and help get Seven out of the car so that they could start working on him. It seemed like only seconds later that a medical team had Seven on a stretcher, rushing him inside the hospital. Paris watched as the doors closed behind them before slowly turning around to get back in the car. She didn't know who shot at her residence, but she vowed she would kill whoever it was. They could have harmed her, Yaseer, or one of the kids if they had been there. She was kind of glad that the kids were spending the night over Erin's house.

"Look, ma... I'm sorry. I had no business showing up on your doorstep like that. But in all honesty, I just missed you. I didn't expect for none of this to go down," Yaseer said in a quiet voice. Inside he was seething. He didn't give to shits about somebody aiming at him, but coming to where his seeds and heart laid their heads was a whole different ball game.

"I'ma drop you off at Erin's and I'll scoop by in the morning to get y'all. I don't care what you say. You're coming back home. I will crash with either Liam, Kai'yan, or Zyon so you can be comfortable. But at least with you there, I can kind of keep an eye on things so that I know y'all are safe. I can't lose y'all, too, P," Yaseer spat with a hint of sadness filling his last few words.

Paris listened to the sincerity of Yaseer's words before responding.

"Yaseer, as much as I'm pissed at you for how you acted tonight, I will not kick you out of your home, no matter how pissed I am at you. I watched you work day in and day out to get where you are today so that you could afford the luxury of your house. So with that being said, we will crash with you until this issue is resolved. Then, once this situation is taken care of for good, we will go back home. I will sleep in one of the guest rooms," Paris replied.

Yaseer nodded his head as he let the words that had just came out of her mouth penetrate his skull. He was glad that she was cool with him staying at the house with them. If he was honest with himself, he was grateful to whatever idiot tried to run up on him, because it brought his family back home, even if it was only temporary.

Chapter 24

By the next morning, Yaseer had pretty much all the answers that he needed to proceed with his plan to take care of the masterminds who were behind everything he and his team had been through for almost two years. And to find out who helped create all the pain and suffering they had been through was shocking. He would have never in a million years thought that the people he looked at like family, loved with all of his heart, and would kill and die for could do him so dirty, but it was cool. It just showed him why he had to continue being what he had been since he was a youngin', a heartless thug.

Yaseer pulled up to the warehouse, parked his car, then just sat idle for a few moments, looking at the building where he had been bringing people for years and sending them off to meet their maker in the worst possible ways. He thought that maybe the shit that was happening in his life was just finally his karma catching up with him for all the pain and suffering that he had caused in people's lives, including the pain that he had caused to the people that were closest to him without even paying attention to the damage that it had caused. Yaseer turned his car off and got out of it, deciding as he walked that after he dropped these last two bodies, he was going to burn this building to the ground and be done with it. He just wanted to live the rest of his life in peace.

Yaseer swiped a hand over his face and exhaled once before he stepped inside, as he often did when he was stressed.

He walked down the hall to the last room, which he considered to be one of the worst torture rooms. It was a cruel way to die.

It was a cremation room. The only difference was that the poor folk who were cremated in there were sedated with Succinylcholine, also known as SUX, to paralyze every muscle in their body, including the muscles that helped them breath, then they were cremated right afterwards. And for the ones who didn't die from suffocation after being injected with the SUX, they were fully alive when they went in, without even the ability to scream. Yaseer checked to make sure that everything was in place and ready to go for that night before walking back out and locking the door to the room.

Yaseer walked back out to his car, making sure the Chambers was secure before he left. As soon as he started his car, his phone started vibrating. Yaseer pulled his phone out and smiled at the caller.

"Hey, ma," Yaseer greeted.

"Hey, son, I was just calling to check on ya."

"I'm gucci, just tryna survive out here in this cruel world, ma. Shoot, I thought you had disappeared on a nigga. What happened to you coming by yesterday?"

"That's the other reason I wanted to call you. I meant to call you yesterday to let you know that I wasn't going to be able to make it because something came up, but I wanted to come through today and spend time with everyone."

"Everyone?" Yaseer questioned as he pulled off from the Chambers.

"Yes, everyone. I haven't really gotten the chance to spend time with everyone since I got out."

"Okay, cool. I'll get everyone together. Is eight o'clock a decent time for you?"

"Yep. Perfect timing. Talk to you later, son," she responded before disconnecting the call.

"Everything is set. They won't even know what hit em," she spat to her lover as she sat cowgirl style on top of him.

***

"So what's the plan Seer?" Zyon questioned as he stepped inside of Yaseer's house.

"Well, I'm pretty sure that she thinks she has the drop on us, but I already got my manz in place to keep me with the 411 until it's time to rock dat ass to sleep, bruh," Yaseer spat as he shook up with Zyon then followed him to the living room where Liam, Erin, and Paris were sitting with the kids.

"Alright, cool, cool. What time is she supposed to get here?"

"In about an hour, bbuuuttt something tells me that she will get here earlier than that," Yaseer replied after he looked down at his Rolley briefly.

"A'ight, cool, you know I'm ready for whatever, big bruh," Zyon said as he sat down on the love seat. "Sup, y'all," he greeted.

"None much, just ready to get this lil situation shakin' and bakin'," Liam replied.

"I must say, though, out of all the people we have taken down, this is one I'm not looking forward to. I mean, how do you look the person you love dead in the eye and kill them? Like, that's some real heartless shit," Yaseer spat.

"No more heartless than what we did to Ezra. Hell, that muhfucka was damn near flesh and blood," Liam replied.

"True, but this still feels a little different for me. Like, that was hurtful, but damn, this feel like a muhfucka ripping my soul out with their bare hands," Yaseer responded.

"I feel ya, bruh," Zyon said as he turned his head at the sound of someone knocking on the front door. He watched as his twin got up to answer the door and shook his head. Some real shit was about to go down.

"Sup, L," everyone greeted as London walked into the living room.

"Sup, shawty," Liam said as he got up, walked up to her, and gave her a hug. "You ready?"

"Yup, more than ever. Everything's already in place. Let's kill dis bitch," London spat with her face turned upward.

"Let's go," Yaseer replied as he checked his extended clip. He was ready for war. Dressed in all-black, the crew left out with only one thing on their mind. Murder.

"Aye, yo, E, if you need me, just call that number that I gave you to reach me and one of us will answer," Yaseer said as he climbed in his blacked out Charger.

"Got cha, broski," she said as she climbed in her whip and drove off, followed by the crew, going in a different direction.

One by one, the crew pulled up to the Chambers, more than ready to send this bitch back to the gates of hell.

Yaseer made a brief stop at Kai'yan's to make sure everything was still going as planned, and just as he thought, it was. Seeing that all was good, Yaseer pulled off and made his way to the Chambers.

Yaseer walked into the Chambers clapping his hands to let everyone know that the package was on the way. They didn't have long to wait before the doors to the warehouse opened. Everyone was kind of tense as they watched Kai'yan walk into The Chambers with Mrs. Davis over his shoulder gagged and tied. Yaseer could see her squirming and putting up a fuss. He was just ready to get this over with.

"Sit her down, big homie," Yaseer spat as he watched Kai'yan sit her down and tie her to the chair.

"Once all of THT is here, we will start this shit," Yaseer said over his shoulder as he took a brief walk down the hall.

Yaseer squatted down and rested his head in his hands. Out of all the kills he had to do in his life, he could barely keep his composer to kill the one person who gave life to him. What kind of person could look their own parent in the face and kill them? He had done some sick shit, but this was by far the sickest, and it was for this reason alone he wanted every member of THT there so that they could see that he didn't even show mercy when it came to his own momma.

Yaseer felt a hand on his shoulder and looked up into the beautiful face of Paris. Looking at her felt like a breath of fresh air and eased his mind. With her by his side, he knew that he could damn near do anything in life, no matter how hard it was. He made a vow that once all this shit was over, he was going to marry Paris. She had stuck with him through a lot. So come hell or high water, he was going to give her the life that she deserved. Yaseer stood up and wrapped his arms around Paris. He needed her strength so that he could get through this one last kill. This had to be the sickest joke that karma could ever play on him.

"Let's go, killa," Paris said above a whisper as she took his hand and walked him back towards the room that held his mom, making sure to drop his hand once they walked in. She didn't want him looking weak in any way, shape, or fashion in this moment.

Yaseer looked over the room, and everyone was in attendance all the way down to his corner boys.

"Take the gag out," Yaseer ordered as he walked to the front of the room, briefly gazing at the open black coffin before turning his back to it and facing the woman that birthed him. Yaseer looked down and was quiet for a brief second before speaking.

"You know, when I was little, I thought there was nothing on this earth that could compare to you. And when you and pops got knocked, it hurt me almost as bad as burying my sister. So never in my life did I think that I would be the one to take your life, but yet here we are. But before I do so, please, mom, just please explain to me why you caused me so much grief and pain. What have I ever done to you to make you hate me so much that you would try your hardest to have me and the people that I love killed?" Yaseer questioned raising his voice just a little. He just didn't understand how a mother could be so cruel to the child that she carried and gave life to.

"Yaseer, you just don't get it, do you?" she spat as she looked him up and down.

"Nope."

"Everything I did was to protect you."

"From who, you? Hold up, before this bitch spit some lies to save her sorry ass life, let me get up there so she can look me in the eyes when she tells them," Eric spat as he walked into the room and up to the front where Yaseer stood.

"Sorry I'm late, son," Eric said he shook up with Yaseer and stood by his side in front of the woman that he once loved with every fiber in his being. Lauren's eyes got big as she looked at Eric standing in front of her, looking good enough to eat. But underneath all of that was a pure dog that only gave two shits about getting his dick wet, and his son was just like him, not giving a damn who they hurt in the process as long as they got they few little precious feel good moments. She could feel her blood starting to boil.

This nigga really has his nerve, she thought to herself before deciding there was no reason to even try to lie now. Hell, she couldn't. Since she had known Eric, she could never lie to him. No matter what, he could always tell when she was lying.

"Y'all niggas always think the sun rises and sets on y'all asses, don't it?" she questioned as she looked back and forth between them.

"Yup, I sure do. Now answer my fuckin' question. Why, mom? Why? What kind of hateful vindictive bitch would try to kill her own son?"

"This bitch right here," Lauren yelled back. "Do you think I didn't struggle with this? But after I heard about you having the little bastards on Paris, just like Mr. Friendly Dick over here did to me, I knew I had to put a stop to it. And the only way I could think to do that was to kill you, just like I did that little bastard of his. No woman deserves to go through the shit that I went through, holding a nigga down day in and down out, risking your life only for him to pay you back with pain." Yaseer stopped listening after hearing her say just like she had done with that little bastard of his.

"Come again?" Yaseer spat, feeling his heartbeat speed up. He was sure that he had heard her wrong. He had to.

"You heard me loud and clear. All it took was the right amount of Benjamins and the right amount of tranexamic acid in her IV, and boom, she wa-" Before Yaseer or Eric could react, Kai'yan had his hands around her throat.

"You fucking crazy ass bitch, you killed my wife! You killed her! You killed her!" Kai'yan kept repeating, looking deranged. It took Yaseer, Eric, Liam, and Zyon to pull him off of her and hold him back from going at her again. Lauren coughed as she tried to catch her breath. She had forgotten who was in the room when she let that little line slip out of her mouth. It took everything within Yaseer to control the beast within.

What kind of woman had he been raised by that would go so far as to have a woman she helped raise killed.

"You know what? You ain't even gotta say shit else," Yaseer said as he walked over to the casket he had out, followed by Eric, who helped him move the casket over to where Lauren was sitting. Then they picked her up, squirming and all, and placed her in the casket, deciding to forgo the SUX meds to paralyze her. He wanted her to try and fight her way out until she took her last breath. Yaseer closed the casket with her screaming and all.

"Help me put this casket onto the machine, pops," Yaseer requested.

"Alright, Kai, come on. You can send her ass off. So we can move on to bigger shit," Yaseer spat.

Kai'yan was overly eager to send her too, which was what he did.

"Follow me," Yaseer ordered as he walked across the hall to another room, which was just as deadly as the room they had just left. Once again, Yaseer stood front and center.

"Now, although my moms had a lot to do with all the turmoil that has been going on in the past and lately, I know she wasn't in it alone. She had help. That's the only way she could have even been able to conjure up half the trouble she caused. So with the being said, I'm going to give this person one chance and one chance only to step forward and take this shit like a G," Yaseer spat as he put his hands in his pocket and looked down. To him, this was going to be almost as hard as killing his mom. But in his eyes and in the eyes of true G's, disloyalty was unforgivable. There were no ifs, ands, or buts about it. Everyone looked over their shoulders, eager to figure out who the traitor was.

"If I have to come drag you out, I promise I will make the way my moms just took a one way trip to hell look like a damn walk in the fucking park," Yaseer threatened as tears graced the rims of his eyes. He just wanted to get this over with before he lost his heart to do so.

Knowing it was no use to delay the inevitable, London stepped forward. She knew her time would come, but she was so hoping that her unborn would at least make it to take its first breath before her number was pulled.

"I don't even want to hear your explanation as to why you pulled the bullshit you did to help my moms, and whoever else, pull the stunts y'all did. You almost succeeded in killing me, not once, but damn near three times, and for what? All because y'all was in your feelings about what went on in *my* fuckin' relationship? Something that had nothing to do with y'all," Yaseer yelled as he stepped to London.

"It had everything to do with me! Any time it comes to my sister, it will always have something to do with me. You kept walking all over her like it didn't mean shit! Y'all men kill me thinking y'all are God's gift to women. I watched my sister stress over you to the point where she miscarried, and yo punk ass didn't even know she was pregnant! It was me who had to hear all of her cries over your constant infidelities. It was me who was there for her when she got knocked because of you and served *yo* time because you wasn't man enough to take your time like a real OG. You didn't and never will deserve my sister, and I hope to God on everything I love yo ass rot in hell for the heartache that you caused her. So yeah, you right, I wanted your ass dead so that she would be better off and at least have a chance at happiness! But yo stubborn ass just wouldn't die!" London spat.

None of the crew could believe their ears. Liam and Paris were more shocked than anyone. Liam had already warned her a while back not to question or come at his brother sideways or she would pay with her life. Love or no love, this would be the first time he would not intervene to save her. In his eyes, she was a snake. She looked in Yaseer's face every day and, instead of expressing her feelings or concerns to him, she got in cahoots with Lauren, Jillian, Ariel, and Ezra to try and take down his brother, no matter whose lives were ruined in the process.

"Hold up. So you mean to tell me you helped caused all this shit as a crusade to try and save me from him?" Paris questioned as she walked up to London with her fist balled up ready for battle.

"I could have died behind Ezra's antics because of you," Paris spat as she punched London in the face, causing London to stumble as blood squirted everywhere from her split lip.

"My daughters could have died because of yo stupid ass," Paris screamed as she took her size eight Timberland boot and kicked London in her stomach, causing London to double over in pain from the forceful kick.

"It wasn't supposed to go that far. It got out of hand. I tried to stop it, I swear, but it was too late."

"You think I give a flying fuck about you trying to stop shit when you helped cause it?" Paris yelled. She stood over London, who was now on her knees with her arms wrapped around her abdomen.

"Paris, please, I'm, I'm pregnant," London muttered out. Paris shook her head.

"Look at it like this, I'm doing it a favor by keeping a low down dirty snake from raising it, and only because of the fact you're pregnant will I make this shit easy!" Paris spat as she pulled her nine before anyone could act and pulled the trigger, sending London off to meet her maker.

Yaseer couldn't even say anything, because it was the same thing he had planned on doing. He couldn't even bring himself to torture her. He was glad that Paris intervened when she did. Yaseer looked over at his brother with pleading eyes to let him know that he was sorry.

A tear dropped as Liam looked back at his brother and nodded his head. Understanding that today's killings were a necessary evil to prevent any future evil didn't help ease the pain that he felt in his heart. But in time, he knew he would eventually heal.

Paris swiped an errant tear from her face as she handed Yaseer her piece and walked out of the building. She needed to get some air. This had been a little too much for her to handle. As soon as Paris walked outside, she couldn't do anything but place her hand on the wall and puke her soul up. She didn't want to have to kill the only person whom she had known better than anyone else, her own flesh and blood. But she would have never trusted her around her or the kids anymore, nor would she have been sure that she wouldn't try to endanger their lives again with more drama and death if she or Yaseer had let her live. So she did what she had to do and put her sister out of her misery. Paris' head turned towards the door as the front door flew open. Yaseer looked to the left then the right before spotting her.

"Oh, babe, I'm so, so sorry," Yaseer said slightly above a whisper as he walked over to Paris and pulled her into his arms. Both of them had taken major losses today, and he knew that things would forever be different for both of them.

Less than three hours later, the Chambers was cleaned and cleared out. Yaseer finally got in his car, along with Paris, cranked it, backed up, pressed a button on a black remote in his car, and sped off as fast as he could before hearing the loud boom from the bombs he had just set off in the Chambers, making sure to burn away any evidence or existence of what used to be. Today was the day that he was finally putting all of this behind him and moving on with his life.

Epilogue
One year later…

"And I now pronounce you man and wife. You may now kiss the bride," the minister said.

Yaseer leaned down and kissed Paris. It took a lot of hard work to win her back, but she was finally his wife. Yaseer looked out over the crowd at the people he called family and his heart smiled.

Liam had met a female that used to work at Yaseer's strip club named Cutie, who was actually pretty good with technology and tracking down folk and info. It was because of her Yaseer was able to get all the info he needed on his mom and London. They were a few months shy from welcoming a beautiful baby girl into the world, whom they had decided they would name Brooklyn, in honor of her aunt.

His dad was there with the attorney that Yaseer had hired to help get him out. They had hooked up and found love.

Kai'yan also had found love in the nanny he had hired to watch after Missy. And Zyon had taken over Yaseer's drug empire and crews, which he ruled with an iron fist, just as Yaseer had. Even Seven, who had made a full recovery from the shoot-out at Paris' house, was there to witness in their union. Yaseer's heart swelled with pride. He was overjoyed with love and happiness as he looked out over everyone and saw his loved ones happy.

This was what he called *Boss 'N Up* in life.

The End.

Here's a sneak peek for THUGS CRY 3 by Ca$h

CHAPTER
1

"**I**'m here! Where you at, pussy boy?" CJ's voice echoed loudly and carried with it a tone of deadly drama.

His eyes bounced off of the many shades of discolored bricks around the infamous government housing projects known as Little Bricks. The boarded-up windows and condemned units, which once housed life, was now a portal for death. Today would give the city a chilling blast from the past, when gunplay and murder was an everyday occurrence.

There was no sight of his nemesis, Nard, but CJ could feel that bitch nigga'z presence in the air as surely as he felt death lurking around every corner.

This is what it had come down to. Under any other circumstances, CJ would have made them niggas come to him and then served them ice cold revenge. But Nard had forged the upper hand by snatching up CJ's brother from another, Raheem, and holding him captive.

CJ was desperate to reverse that shit.

Hot surges passed rapidly through his body as he thought of how somewhere, bound and gagged, Raheem was hostage to those grimy ass niggas and he knew they would surely kill him if he hadn't shown up.

It's do or die, CJ mumbled through clenched teeth. He took one last glance up toward Heaven where his girl, Tamika, rested in paradise, offering a few words. *See you in a minute, shorty.*

He lowered his gaze and then looked deep into the crevices of the buildings. "Where ya punk ass at? Show yo face, coward muhfucka," he called out again.

"I'm right here, bitch nigga. Look around, I'm not hard to find!" Nard stepped out of the apartment that he'd been hiding in.

He had Raheem in front of him like a human shield. One hand held Raheem by the back of the collar, while the other held a Glock Nine to the back of his head, locked and loaded. If CJ flinched, he was gonna put his man's noodles on the pavement.

CJ knew how Nard got down. His trigger finger itched to put something hot in his chest but there was no way to wet Nard without bodying Raheem, too. That was a risk he was unwilling to take because if it hadn't been for his mistakes, his man wouldn't be in that position.

Fuck! CJ snorted under his breath. He couldn't believe he had let a little young nigga, like Nard, gain the ups on him. Not after all the muhfuckaz he'd gone to war with and prevailed over on the road to riches and hood fame.

There has to be a way to flip the script and regain the upper hand, CJ thought.

Sensing that CJ was contemplating letting his gun roar, Nard tightened his grip on Raheem's collar and ducked further down behind him. A quick shift of his eyes confirmed his shooters were in place, and on point. He spotted them, clad in black, lined up in several doorways. If CJ tried anything, they were going to Swiss cheese his ass.

CJ had already surveyed the area. He saw gunners posted up in breezeways, behind partially cracked doors and on the rooftop of the building Nard had exited. None of that worried him, though. His only concern was Raheem.

He cursed himself for allowing his fam to get involved in the beef between him and Nard, as he faced what could be his final moments.

Raheem sat at the bar inside of CJ's crib out in New Haven, Connecticut. His elbows rested on the counter top with his hands steepled under his chin. Despite grieving the suicide of

Sparkle, his only true love, Raheem was concerned about what CJ was going through.

Nard had murdered CJ's girl, Tamika, her mom and her cousin. He could see the pain in CJ's face, and he knew retaliation was a must. The way CJ was built there was no way he wouldn't avenge that shit.

And there was no way Raheem would let his mans go to war without him at his side.

"Just give me the game plan, my brotha. You know I'm gonna ride," he said.

"Nah, fam, I'ma handle it myself. The streets ain't your life anymore." Raheem was one of the few that had made it out of The Bricks and had done something legitimate with his life. "I'm not lettin' you return to the very shit you moved away to escape from," stated CJ, adamantly.

But Raheem was too loyal to be dissuaded. He looked his best friend in the eyes and replied, "CJ, this ain't about the game. This ain't about The Bricks either. You're my brotha from a different mother, and what hurts you, hurts me. When you bleed, I bleed."

"Fam, I can't let you do it." CJ stood firm.

"And you can't stop me either," he said with conviction that was unwavering.

In the end, CJ had relented and his dawg had rode shotgun, never voicing a regret. Not even when CJ's ego caused him to make a crucial mistake.

CJ replayed it all in his mind, in a nano-second, as he looked at Raheem with regret. Their bond was from the cradle to the grave, but Rah's life deserved a much better ending.

Over Raheem's shoulder, Nard flashed a gloating smile. CJ sneered at him and spat on the ground. Even from the distance of about twenty feet that separated them, CJ could see that his mans had been severely beaten. One of his eyes was swollen completely shut, blood covered his face and his body seemed limp.

An intense pang shot through CJ's heart and the blood in his veins boiled hotter than lava. "Let him go," he belted.

Surrounded by a small army, Nard felt invincible. "Let him go?" He laughed smugly. "Nah, it ain't gonna be that easy, blood. I'ma find out how low your nuts hang." He slid a gun from his waist and held it down at his side.

"They hang to the muhfuckin' ground, nigga! You see I'm here. I ain't scared to die," spat CJ.

"We'll see," said Nard.

"You'll see? Nigga, you can see right now." CJ ripped his shirt off and pounded his chest with a fist. "I'm the muhfuckin' best that ever did it!" he proclaimed with the defiant arrogance that had propelled him to the top of the drug game.

But Nard was just as egotistical. And fueled by a deep hatred of CJ, that had escalated the night CJ made Tamika clown him in front of a club full of people, he was determined to make CJ bow down. "You can't be the best when there's only one of me," he slung back.

"Young boy, you're a *Cam'ron* wannabe. Fuck you saying? How are you the best hiding behind the next nigga? Let him go and let's play with these tools," CJ challenged. "Just you and me. Show me how low your little ass nuts hang."

"This how low they hang, fuck nigga!" Nard barked. He placed the gun against Raheem's leg.

Boom!

***

Inside of a gutted-out unit, that had been 26-year old Shabazz' home for the past two weeks, he had heard the loud gunshot. He hopped up off of the floor and quickly stepped into his rundown Timbs. He walked past a milk crate, that served as his dining table, and hurried to the window to see what the fuck was going on.

His first thought was that those punk ass Newark cops were chasing squatters and dope fiends away, who took refuge inside of the dilapidated apartments to get away from the cold temperatures that had dropped into the low 40's as of last night. *But why would five-oh be busting shots at homeless people?* he wondered.

As Shabazz made his way to the front window, he heard the unmistakable bark of street niggaz embroiled in a heated exchange, that increased by the second. He moved to the side to gain a better look through a space between the boards, that covered most of the window. From his shaded view, he scanned the area in an attempt to ID one of them.

"Fuck!" Shabazz said as he strained to get a better look.

He glanced over to his far right to see a sleek, black sports car parked haphazardly in the middle of the street, with the driver's door swung wide open.

Shabazz didn't have to guess who the expensive whip belonged to. He knew of only one person in the hood who drove a Maybach.

"CJ! What the fuck is going on?" Shabazz squinted.

When his sights set on Newark's most notorious drug dealer, Cam'ron Jeffries, standing bare-chested beside the Maybach, bouncing from foot to foot, boisterously, he knew, then, shit was about to be catastrophic.

Shabazz repositioned himself to see CJ yelling at Nard, the young hustler who was making a name for himself in The Bricks.

He didn't know Nard personally, but he had seen him around the city on many occasions. Secretly, he admired what he had been able to accomplish in the game at such a young age. But what Shabazz felt for CJ was beyond admiration, it bordered on idolization.

Shabazz wasn't a dick rider, but he had no problem saluting a man's accomplishments. He knew firsthand how hard it was to rise from the dirt up. CJ had done that and a whole lot more.

In The Bricks his name was legendary, and like most other kingpins that had come before him, it was inevitable that some young wolf would come for his crown.

Shabazz shook his head at the fatalistic results that we're about to be played out, right before his very eyes. Two beasts, both with indomitable wills, stood in the middle of the street, locked in a tangle with steel and bad intent. He was certain one or both of them would end up dead.

Pressing his unshaven face further against the window, he watched the deadly drama unfold.

***

CJ fought back the urge to raise his arm and let his tool spit. The level of testosterone that flowed through his body was barely containable. He felt in his heart that he could take on Nard and his punk ass crew and walk up out of Little Bricks with all of their blood on his hands. But Rah would certainly get caught in the crossfire, if Nard didn't kill him as soon as the first shot rang out from CJ's strap.

Fuck it! I'm not risking my peeps' life, CJ decided. He mean mugged Nard, who was still shielding himself with Raheem's body.

CJ let his finger ease off of the trigger. He spread his arms out wide and shouted, "Fuck you wanna do? Stand here all day tryna build up the courage to kill me? "

Nard smirked. "I'm not gon' kill you. I'ma make you murk ya'self. If you love your man and want me to let him go, eat your gun, bitch ass nigga. Take ya'self outta the game."

Fuck no! Shabazz said to himself as he watched on. He had no way of knowing how trill CJ and Rah's bond was, but he suspected Nard would kill CJ's boy regardless. *Might as well go out with your banger poppin'. Take a few niggaz to Hell wit'chu. Real shit.*

CJ unzipped his pants and pulled his wood out. "It's all dick over here." He took a piss in Nard's direction. "This is what I think of you and your bitch ass crew."

Behind the window, Shabazz covered his mouth with his hand to keep from cheering. "That nigga, CJ, hard as fuck!" he whispered.

Nard wasn't impressed. "You think I'm playin' with you?" he yelled. Then, to reinforce his cold bloodedness he shot Rah again.

"Ahhhh!" This time Rah cried out in excruciating pain as the hot, sizzling bullet tore through his insides. Blood ran from his body and into the freshly planted snow. He curled up within himself and groaned heavily as beads of sweat formed on his forehead, despite the chilling cold.

Nard smiled menacingly. "I'ma make him suffer," he taunted CJ.

Rah winced as the pain from the gunshot set his insides ablaze. Somehow he summoned up the strength to yell to CJ. "Kill this nigga, yo!"

CJ, who had murdered mercilessly over and over again, couldn't bare seeing his main mans suffer, but his nemesis showed no mercy.

Nard pressed his heat to the back of Raheem's head and sent a chilling stare back CJ's way. "It's either him or you. Eat that gun, nigga, before I release all your mans' brains over here."

For some unexplainable reason, witnessing this, Shabazz snatched his Nine off of his waist. Their beef had nothing at all to do with him, but he was ready to thrust himself dead in the middle of it. But a quick glance at all of the gunners, whom he had concluded must've been down with Nard, made Shabazz think better of it.

"Let him go, he served his purpose. This is between me and you," he heard CJ bellow.

"Do it! Pull the trigger and end yo' life, and I'll spare your mans'," said Nard.

Shabazz shook his head *no*, as if CJ could see him.

"Lil' punk muhfucka," he screamed at Nard. "You think you're saying something? Huh? Huh?"

In the middle of the snow covered street, CJ remained gangsta. He stood up on his toes and bounced from foot to foot, full of adrenaline. His tatted chest heaved up and down, and his arms flung out at his sides. Instead of cowering, he embraced the ultimatum like the real nigga he had always professed to be.

"Kill ya'self or I'm slaying ya mans, B. This is your last chance." Nard retorted.

"Nigga, fuck you. You ain't saying shit! I'm G'd up 'til my feet up. I'll die for my nigga. Can you say that, punk muthafucka?" CJ shoved his gun in his own mouth.

Shabazz' eyes grew big. This was like something he would see in a cinema, only it wasn't a movie. This was real life. "Nooo, son, don't do it," he mumbled.

Boom!

The single gunshot sounded like a loud clap of thunder. Shabazz stared in disbelief as CJ's head exploded in a spray of red and his body crumpled to the ground.

"Oh, fuck!" Shabazz' mouth was left wide open and his head shook from side to side.

166

He watched as Nard let CJ's boy fall to the ground. A second later, several of the men that had been posted up, watching Nard's back, appeared at his side. One by one, they walked over to where CJ's body lay sprawled out on the ground and pumped an exclamation shot in his corpse.

Shabazz didn't like that at all. *He's already dead. Why y'all gotta disrespect him like that? Regardless of y'all beef, that nigga was a street legend. You don't do him like that!* His brow knitted and his mouth was tight. His hand wrapped around his tool, but he wisely chose to stay put, even as he witnessed them pick CJ's body up and toss it in a dumpster like trash.

Shabazz could barely contain his fury. He bit down hard on his lip and took a deep breath, battling back and forth with the voice that calmed the beast resonating within.

Outside, Big Nasty lifted Nard's arm in victory. "It's over, dawg. You're the new king," he anointed.

Nard smiled. "We own The Bricks!" he boasted, and all of his minions applauded.

Y'all bitch niggaz don't own nothin! thought Shabazz. *You didn't murk CJ, he gave his life for his mans. That's real G shit.* He tapped his chest with his fist in salutation.

Beyond the window, Nard stood over the one who CJ had sacrificed his life for. His gun was aimed down at Rah. While his team urged him to empty his clip in him, Nard searched his mind for a way to put his signature on this particular kill because Rah had withstood all forms of torture in refusing to set CJ up.

Nard's brother, Man Dog, could see the wheels turning in his head. "Just do that nigga," he said.

But Nard was on a narcissistic high. "Nah, son, he thinks he's hard. I'ma leave him here to die in the same streets he couldn't leave alone. Or maybe he can crawl in the dumpster and die with his mans."

Man Dog laughed. "You a cold muthafucka."

"Let's go. Fuck 'em!" Nard waved his arm as he headed to the car.

"Yeah, fuck 'em!" They chanted in unison as they spat at Rah's blood soaked body.

With chuckles and banter of their success they all moved out, leaving Rah to die slowly. What they hadn't counted on was his impregnable will to live and extract revenge.

And that's gon' be their demise, thought Shabazz after he raced outside to find Rah still breathing.

CHAPTER
2
Eric

Shit had gotten real in the streets, but I was trained to go. My murder game was official and my attitude was straight gangsta. So, when those niggaz did the unthinkable to Rah, me and the entire crew was ready to send mad heat at 'em

Along the way, something my brother, CJ, once said would be reinforced in all of our minds, over and over again.

"The game is a cold-hearted bitch. It can take you to the highest heights and then sink you to the lowest depths, all in the same day. And no matter how hard a nigga is, if you fuck with the streets long enough, you'll eventually find out that thugs cry, too," he schooled.

Understanding that, we were determined to make sure that our enemies shed the last tears.

Down in the Iron Bound section of Newark, inside a warehouse that had become our headquarters, I knocked on the door to CJ's office but received no answer. At the moment, I had no reason to be concerned. I just figured my brother needed a little time alone.

Like the rest of us, he was real fucked up over Raheem's kidnapping. With each passing day, the stress lines in his face grew deeper. Lately, I could hear the tension in his voice when he spoke. And our failure to find out where Nard was holding Rah compounded all his worries.

The latest pics Nard sent confirmed what we all suspected: Rah was being tortured. But there was no doubt in our minds how Rah would rock. He would choose a bullet in the head over betrayal in the heart. That's just how real he was. Mad niggaz claimed to be about that life, but Raheem lived that shit, 24/7, 365.

On one hand, his unquestionable gangsta fortified us. We could plot our moves without having to worry that he would bitch up and flip. On the other hand, his thoroughness caused us to fear the inevitable—he would refuse to fold and Nard would murk him.

Just thinking about that shit caused me to shake my head in frustration. Rah wasn't family by blood but he was as much of a big brother to me as CJ. Throughout my life, I could count on him in times of need, so his predicament had me vexed.

I let out a long sigh and clenched my fingers tightly. *I need my nigga back.*

The pain in my chest was indescribable. That's how much love I had for Rah. When my brother made that call to Atlanta, asking him to come back to Newark to help us in a street war that had left CJ's girl, Tamika, and her family dead, fam didn't hesitate to gather up a few of his soldiers in the *'A'* and board that flight.

A few days later, with two ATL goons, DaQuan and Legend, accompanying him, Rah arrived in Newark with one thing on his mind—stacking bodies.

Together, we made many mothers mourn their sons.

Legend and DaQuan quickly proved their mettle and we became joined at the hip. But the other side didn't fold. They had managed to slump DaQuan, though, and now that they had Rah captive, all of us was desperate to get him back unharmed.

No one was saying it, but we all knew that the longer those niggas had him, the less likely we would ever see him alive again. We had already lost one real hitta, DaQuan, to their guns, losing Rah would crush us all.

The mere thought of that made my knees weaken. I placed my hands against the sides of the door frame to steady myself.

After straightening my back and shaking that image from my mind, I turned from CJ's office and walked back into the main area of the warehouse. Legend was just returning from making a quick run to the store when I entered the room.

"Sup, my nigga, anything new?" he inquired as he sat large White Castles bags down on a work bench.

"Nah, son, ain't nothin' changed. Those bitch niggaz are still playing cat and mouse," I somberly reported.

"It's all good," Legend nodded his head up and down, "they're about to feel our wrath."

"Say that!" intoned Snoop, who was sitting on a crate cleaning his AK-47 assault rifle.

"Know that!" Premo co-signed our enemies' death warrants as he rose up off of the couch that sat in the middle of the spacious warehouse and walked over to see what Legend had brought back to eat.

Reaching inside the bags, Snoop pulled out burgers, fries and some other sandwiches and passed them around. I unwrapped my chicken sandwich and took a bite. I hadn't eaten in two days but I didn't have an appetite, so I sat the sandwich down on the bench and watched the others eat while my mind replayed everything that had happened since the beef with Nard popped off.

Over several months, both squads had taken losses. We left some of their crew with dirt faces, while they snatched the hearts out of our chests with DaQuan's murder. Nearly three months had passed since that unforgettable day. But when I closed my eyes at night, I still saw vivid images of my dude stretched out on the pavement.

"We gotta hurry up and find these niggas and kill 'em," I blurted out. "They gotta pay in the worst way!"

"Fa sho! I promised DaQuan's girl that I would bury every one of those bitch-made muthafuckas!" Pain resonated from

Legend's voice as he slung his burger across the room. "I'm tired of sitting around waiting to hear from those pussies, I'm ready to wreak havoc around this bitch!" He snatched his machete off of a nearby table and held it down at his side.

"I'm wit'chu, Black." Snoop brows knitted as he chewed on his food.

"All of us are with it, but like CJ said, we gotta move cautiously until we get Rah back, then we can smash everything. No matter what, we can't do anything that might make them kill Rah," said Premo.

I nodded my head in agreement but Legend obviously felt differently. He let out an exasperated sigh. "Man, let's keep it one *hunnid* -- y'all really think Nard is gonna let Rah live, knowing how shorty get down for his?" He looked from Premo to me. "Be real, my nigga, what do you think?"

"I don't know, son. I'm just hoping..." I casted my eyes to the floor and let my voice trail off.

"I got that same hope but I'm also a realist, ain't no way they're letting homie go."

"Fuck is you saying, yo? You trying to say Rah is already dead." I reached out and shoved Legend. I was ready to fight but to his credit he recognized my aggression for what it was, hurt.

"E, ain't nan man in this room love Rah no more than I do. I'll lay my life down for homie. But we can't keep underestimating the opposition, those niggas are killaz too," he said.

"Fuck those pussies!" I spat, refusing to give them any props at all. If they were really about that murder shit, they wouldn't be hiding like a bunch of hoes.

"I feel you. But sitting around waiting for them to call our shots ain't getting Rah back. I say we hit the streets and let our tools spit. Put that bitch nigga, Nard, under so much pressure he'll have no other choice but to release Rah," said Legend.

"That shit sounds good, nah mean? The only problem with that is none of Nard's people are around for us to smash," I reminded him. Like a coward, Nard had ordered all of his drug houses to shut down, and he had pulled his people off of the streets.

"Ho-ass muthafuckaz," spat Legend, echoing my sentiments.

We all grew quiet as a feeling of helplessness washed over the room. I grabbed a few sandwiches off of the table. "I'ma go see if CJ wants something to eat." Feeling mentally weary, I made my way back to his office.

As I reached the door, I thought about what Legend had said. Maybe we did need to turn the heat up on Nard by crushing any and everybody associated with him, regardless to how loose their connection was. But who was I to question my brother's strategy?

CJ had proven, over and over again, that his gangsta was unmatched. His body count exceeded all of ours put together. And in spite of the current situation, he remained my hero.

The others on the team didn't agree with every decision CJ made, though. They felt some of the things he'd done was plain reckless. But that was part of what made him a beast. He was capable of killing on impulse and with no regard.

With his hands still wet with blood, he might hit the club and stunt on muthafuckaz. A body could be in the trunk of his whip and CJ would be in the club popping bottles like he didn't have a worry in the world. Niggaz respected him, but they feared him even more. In my eyes, absolutely no one measured up to him.

Rah was different, though. He was a thinker and much more humble than any of us. And when it came to warfare, son always anticipated the enemy's next move. That's why I had always felt that if anybody got caught slipping, it wasn't gon' be him.

Damn. How did they get you, fam? That was the burning question in my mind.

I stood there tryna fight back a tidal wave of guilt that surged through my heart. If I could turn back the hands of time, I would've never let him leave the club to take Kenisha home without me that night.

"Damn, son, I fucked up!" I leaned my head against the wall outside the door of CJ's office.

Though the guilt I felt was deep, there was no way it measured up to what I imagined my brother was feeling. Him and Rah came up together eating Ramen Noodles off the same fork. CJ had chosen the street life while Rah had made it out, only to be called back to bust his gun at our sides. Now his life was in the enemy's hands.

Deep down, we all knew what the outcome would be, but we weren't ready to accept it. Until Rah's body turned up, I was not gonna lose hope. Because if Allah truly protected the good, my nigga was gonna be a'ight.

Slightly comforted by that thought, I raised my head and knocked on the office door. "CJ you a'ight in there?" I waited for a response but got none.

I knocked again, harder this time, but he still didn't answer. "Bruh, I brought you something to eat," I called out.

When the only response I received was more silence, I turned and walked back up front. Legend and Snoop was huddled together talking in hushed tones. Premo was staring out of a window with his back to everyone. I walked over and placed a hand on his shoulder. I could feel the tenseness in his muscles.

"Anything moving out there?" I asked in a low voice.

Premo replied with a slow shake of his head, that instantly made my blood turn hot. "Nigga, why you acting defeated?" I questioned him in a harsh tone.

"Save that shit, yo! This ain't the right time," he said over his shoulder.

I took a deep breath and let it out slowly. As I contemplated our next move, my mind began to shift to Legend's way of thinking. Sitting back doing nothing was like defanging a wolf. Me and my niggas were killaz, it was time to do what killaz do.

I cleared my voice and looked Premo in the eyes. "You say nothin's moving out there, right?" My voice turned gravelly.

"Nah, son. Not shit," he restated.

"Well, we're about to make some shit move. C'mon, let's go holla at CJ and see if we can get him to take the clamps off of us. It's time to murder some muthafuckaz!" I dropped the food right there on the floor and turned to look at my other mans. What I saw in their eyes reconfirmed my trust in their gangsta.

Legend snatched his machete off of the table and gripped it with force. Earlier, he had used it to chop the hands off of a muthafucka that we suspected of having a role in Rah's kidnapping. He raised the bloody blade in the air and sliced it back and forth. "Fuck cutting off a bitch nigga'z hands, I'm 'bout to decapitate me a bitch!" he vowed.

"That's what the fuck I'm talm 'bout." Premo got crunk. "We gotta remind niggaz who the fuck we be, nah mean."

Snoop whipped out his tool and click-clacked a bullet in the chamber of his fo-five. "Muthafuckaz about to meet their Maker, son. Word!" he proclaimed.

I let a smile play across my face. Now my team was talking the type of shit I needed to hear. If Nard was gonna kill Rah, we had to show him we would retaliate with force.

With a plan formulating in my mind, I led the way to CJ's office to let him know that we wanted to unleash terror in The Bricks. No more waiting! Fuck that chill shit his police connects was talking 'bout. There wouldn't be peace in the streets until Nard and his whole team had tombstones with their names on them.

Knocking on the door again, I said, "Yo, Big Bruh, can we come in?"

This time, when he didn't answer, I stepped forward, turned the knob and pushed the door open. We entered one behind the other. The chair behind CJ's desk was unoccupied and turned backwards, as if he had gotten up in a hurry. My eyes surveyed the office suspiciously. CJ was nowhere in sight and the back door was wide open. The cold November wind whistled through it and rushed up on us in a chilly blast.

"What the fuck?" uttered Snoop.

Legend hurried to the door and peered out into the back lot. "You see his ride?" asked Premo.

"Negative, man, it's gone."

An ominous feeling came over me. I slammed my palms against the door frame and let out a pained cry. "Fuck! They got him! I can feel that shit in my heart, yo."

"Those bitch niggaz ain't got shit!" Snoop disagreed. "There's no fuckin' way they ran up in here and snatched him up without us hearing a sound."

"No muthafuckin' way! CJ would've went out in a blaze, and a coupla them would be laying on this floor beside him," said Legend.

Premo stepped back inside and pulled the door closed. "True story. He probably went looking for Rah on his own. That must be the reason he sent all of us out of his office earlier, so we couldn't stop him from going rogue," he surmised.

That made sense to me. I could picture CJ saying to himself, *Y'all niggaz ain't gotta look for me, I'ma look for you!*

But Nard and 'em couldn't be taken lightly. "We gotta find him, ASAP."

I whipped out my iPhone and made the call. After the phone rang three times, I was sent to voicemail. Panic filled my chest as I hung up and immediately pressed REDIAL. When I was sent to voicemail a second time, a feeling of dread coursed through my body and choked off my breath.

"What up, E?" I could barely make out Premo's voice as I staggered behind the desk and sat down heavily in his chair. I let my head rest on the desktop as tears forced their way into my eyes.

"He ain't answering, yo." I said in a tone muffled by despair.

"Shawdy, what the fuck?" Legend's voice boomed. "Show some faith in your brother's gangsta. You know CJ is about that gunplay as much as anybody. You know he can handle himself in any situation. Wherever he's at, you can bet it's on his own terms."

"I hear you talking." My response held little conviction because my heart told me that CJ was dead.

I lifted my head and wiped my eyes with the heel of my hands. The pain in my heart was indescribable but the thoroughness of my bloodline rose to the surface. I was my brother's keeper and, no matter what, I would not wilt.

"You a'ight, folks?" asked Legend.

"Nah, blood," I answered truthfully, "but it's way too soon to mourn." I stood up from the desk and took charge. "Lock up everything and let's roll out. Snoop, you and Premo ride together. I'ma ride with Legend. Search the whole muhfuckin' city until we find CJ. If my brother is dead, I'ma turn The Bricks blood red."

CHAPTER
3
Eric

After padlocking the back door, we hurried to our cars and went in search of CJ. As Legend drove through the city, keeping an anxious eye out for CJ's Maybach, I continuously called his phone. Each time, it rang a few times before going to voicemail. Finally, I decided to leave a message with extreme urgency in my tone.

"Yo, bruh, answer your phone. You got a nigga worried about you. Hit me back when you get this." I stared at the screen desperately trying to will it to light up with CJ's number, but no call back ever came.

We drove through our spots up and down Clinton Street, asking if any of our block boys had seen him. No one had heard from CJ or knew where he was at nor had they seen any of his whips passing through the hood. Every call we made brought the same response, and Snoop and Premo were encountering the same disheartening answers.

Talking to Premo on the phone, I said, "Y'all head out to East Orange and see if those niggaz out there have seen him. Me and Legend gon' try to find that lil' young broad, Kenisha, that he fuck with. Maybe he's chilling with her, just tryna clear his head."

"Say no more."

I let out a sigh of frustration as I ended the call. I didn't know where Kenisha lived and I doubted CJ would be laid up in some pussy at a time like this, but I had to turn over every stone. "Yo, you know where lil' mama live?" I asked Legend.

"Nah. I just know her pops is an Islamic minister or some shit like that." He stopped at a traffic light at the intersection of Central Avenue and Grove Street.

I leaned my head against the dashboard. "This shit is fucked up!"

"Don't panic, fam. We gon' find him," Legend attempted to reassure me but his confidence did nothing to allay my fear.

I sat up in my seat and I tried calling my brother once more. The phone rang twice and then, finally, someone answered.

"Hello." The voice didn't belong to CJ, though.

I glanced down at the screen to make sure I hadn't dialed the wrong number. When I saw that I hadn't, I got pissed the fuck off! "Who the fuck is this?" I gritted.

Legend's head snapped in my direction. "Is that CJ?" His voice was filled with hope.

I shook my head *no*. On the other end, the man said, "My name is Shabazz. Are you CJ and Rah's people?"

"Fuck is it to you, nigga? Put CJ on the phone," I snapped.

"Blood, if you're his peeps, I got some bad news."

"I'm his people. What bad news you got?" My body slumped down in the seat as I anticipated the worst.

"CJ is dead, man, and Rah is fucked up real bad. I don't think he gon' make it, yo."

"Fuck is you saying, nigga?" I cried as pain and anger gripped me like nothing I had ever felt before. "Play with this shit if you want to and end up in a goddam casket. Put my brother on the phone right muthafuckin' now!" I didn't wanna believe my ears.

The light turned green but Legend didn't move. Horns honked and drivers behind us hurled insults that under any other circumstances, would've got them wet the fuck up. But me and Legend was oblivious to everything outside of the vehicle.

"Bruh, you got five seconds to put CJ on the phone!" I threatened.

"B, you not listening to me, yo. CJ is dead!" Shabazz' voice sounded like it was about to break. "He's dead, man. Those niggaz did him dirty."

"Blood, don't tell me no shit like dat!" I exploded.

"Son, you don't know how bad I wish I didn't have to."

Legend reached over and took the phone from me. "Yo, talk to me, my nigga. What the fuck is going on?" He pulled off and turned into a lot and parked.

"Put that nigga on speaker." I ran a hand down my face to wipe the flood of hot tears that poured from my eyes.

Legend took the phone away from his ear and put it on speaker. Shabazz said, "Yo, son, I don't know you but since y'all calling CJ's phone, I guess you're who you say you are. Like I said, CJ is dead, and ol' boy did him real foul. Your mans, Rah, is barely alive. They fucked him up real bad, yo. That's all I'ma say on the phone. Just meet me at University. The ambulance is rushing Rah there now. Hurry up!"

The line went dead. Legend just let the phone fall from his hand. He dropped his head against the steering wheel and mumbled incoherently as we both tried to process the man's words.

"Ain't no way in hell my brother is dead. *Not CJ.* I refuse to believe that!"

"Damn, my nigga, this some bullshit." Legend slowly raised his head and looked at me. Unspilled tears brimmed his eyes. "I can't even think," he said, barely above a whisper.

I couldn't think clearly, either. The news had shattered my world but until I saw proof that my brother was dead, I refused to accept it. "Fam, we gotta go to the hospital to see if what he was saying is true," I spoke in a broken tone.

As Legend drove to University, we both held on to hope that my brother wasn't dead. "That was some bullshit, shawdy. Them niggaz ain't done killed CJ. This is some type of set up.

But if they think we ain't gon' show up, they got the game fucked up," he spewed.

My head was all fucked up and I couldn't stop the tears from falling from eyes. Somehow, I managed to call Premo. As soon as he answered, I told him the business.

"How the fuck could that happen?" He was bewildered. But the fact that Shabazz answered CJ's phone led him to believe it had to be true. "And if it was a setup, they wouldn't want us to meet them at the hospital. They would know that Hot Top be all around that bitch," he said, meaning the police.

"Yeah, you're right," I agreed. "I'm still not believing that shit until I see it with my own eyes. Meet us at the hospital. Man, I'm telling you if this shit is true I'm going on a mutha-fuckin' rampage!"

"Me too." Like mine, his voice was strained with emotion.

I hung up the phone and glanced at Legend through my tears. His jaw was set and his eyes burned fiery. But when he glanced back at me and spoke, his country voice was calm. "Shawdy, we don't know nothin' yet. Whatever the outcome, though, we not gon' fold. You understand me?" he said with conviction.

I just nodded my head. For a long moment, we rode in complete silence. As we got closer to the hospital, reality punched me in the chest. Who the fuck was we trying to fool other than ourselves? "He's gone, yo. Them bitch ass niggaz killed my brother. I can feel it in my soul."

I silently prayed that I was wrong. But in my heart of hearts, I knew that I wasn't. All I could do was hope that Rah wasn't dead, too.

CHAPTER
4
Eric

As soon we pulled into the hospital's parking lot, Legend found a vacant parking space. I hopped and hurried inside with him right on my heels.

A nigga'z heart was pounding hard as hell as I walked through the Emergency Room doors. Inside it was mad pandemonium. Tragedy or some form of worry was etched on every face I looked into.

"Noooo, not my baby!" screamed a heavy-set, black woman with a dirty scarf tied around her head. A doctor in a white lab coat tried to comfort her, but she started fighting him. "You let my baby die!" she cried.

The word *die* rung in my ears on repeat. Was my brother really dead? I wanted to close my eyes, blink twice, and wake up from this nightmare. But the fact of the matter was this was not a dream. Those were real tears pouring down my face, and real worry sizzling through my body as I pushed passed a horde of people in a desperate rush to reach the front desk and get some answers.

Legend was a few steps in front of me, slinging mutha-fuckaz out of our way. As we emerged from the crowd of people in the ER, I noticed a familiar face. It was Paris, a homegirl from Little Bricks, who worked at the hospital. A few years ago, she had been one of my brother's side chicks.

Our eyes met and I hurried up to her. "What's up, ma? Tell me what's going on. Did they bring CJ here?" I asked in a harried tone.

"No, but they brought Raheem in."

Legend leaned in from behind me. "Is he gonna make it?" he asked.

"I don't know. I heard one of the other nurses talking and she sounded doubtful." Paris choked up.

Legend's head dropped to his chest, and my knees buckled. *No, not Rah.* This shit was bad. I titled my head to the sky and silently sent a prayer up for my nigga, hoping he would pull through.

Finding the strength to stand up straight and face the truth, however painful it might be, I steadied my legs and asked Paris, "What about my brother?"

She looked at me for a second, and then she lowered her eyes to the floor. Angrily, I reached up, grabbed her by the face with both hands and forced eye contact. Tears trailed down her face and she fell into my arms sobbing. That's when I knew for sure that CJ was gone. I just wanted confirmation.

"Paris!" I held her away from me and shook her violently. "Stop crying and answer my question!" But no matter how hard I shook her, she just couldn't force the words out of her mouth.

Legend stepped up and barked in her face. "Answer him! Is CJ dead?"

Before she could pull herself together and stamp our fears true, I felt a hand on my shoulder. I released Paris and spun around quickly. Standing there was a dark skinned dude who was rocking a light, scraggly beard, a gray coat and a black hoodie. I knew who he was before he identified himself.

"I'm Shabazz, yo. You're Eric, CJ's little brother, right?" He held his hand out for some dap, but until I knew for sure he was official, I was treating him with suspicion, so I left his fist hanging.

"Yeah, I'm his brother. How do you know me?"

"I used to trap on Hawthorne before I went away on a lil' bid. You and CJ used to come through there sometime."

I studied his face for a minute and suddenly I recalled seeing him around our spot he had mentioned. My suspicions eased up a little but this wasn't a reunion. I needed to know what had happened to my brother.

"Give it to me raw, yo. Is my brother dead?" I asked.

Shabazz slowly nodded his head up and down. "Yeah, fam. I'm sorry to have to tell you that. But if it's any consolation, he went out real gangsta."

He kept on talking but I barely heard another word. My body slumped as I tried to envision living on without my heart. My brother was everything to me, and know they were telling me he's gone. "Are you sure?" I asked again.

Shabazz nodded *yes* a second time, and then Paris removed all doubt. Sniffling back more tears, she said, "The paramedics that brought Rah in said it was bad. I didn't see CJ's body because they took him straight to the coroner's. But I knew it had to be him because they described CJ's Maybach..."

I put my hand up to cut her off. I didn't want to hear nothing else until I gathered myself. Legend threw an arm around my shoulders and gave me a brotherly hug.

"It's gon' be a'ight," he consoled.

"No, it's not. But it's damn sure about to get ugly," I replied bitterly.

"I'm wit' dat." His tone mirrored mine.

When I looked up, I saw Premo and Snoop coming through the door, followed by a half dozen or so of our foot soldiers. I could tell from their aggressive postures that each one of them was strapped and ready to bang on an opponent. Cops were all around the place, and their eyes followed Snoop 'nem all the way over to us.

I G-hugged Premo first, then Snoop.

"What's the business?" Snoop asked, looking at me with sad eyes.

I knew what he was asking, and my answer came out tinged with the pain that was in my heart. "He's gone, bruh. Those bitch ass niggaz killed him." I reached up and caught a falling tear with the back of my hand.

"It's killing season!" Snoop gritted.

"Shh!" Legend quickly put his finger up to his lips, urging us to tone down. "Fam, the po's are all over this bitch and they're sweating us hard. "Let's step outside."

We all looked up and saw Newark's Finest eyes beamed in on us. As we turned and headed outside, I said to Shabazz, "You come, too." I wanted the rest of the crew to hear, first-hand, the story he had to tell.

Outside, we stood in a circle with the wind whistling around us as Shabazz replayed what had happened, blow by blow. Each word that left his mouth brought a tear from my eyes. In my mind, I drew a vivid picture of the events as he detailed them. Everything he recounted personified the bond CJ and Rah shared, and although I was hurting bad inside, my chest swelled with pride knowing that my brother had given his life for his partner. I couldn't be mad at him for that because I had no doubt Rah would've done the same for him.

What made my blood boil was when Shabazz told us how Nard had thrown CJ's body in a dumpster and proclaimed himself to be the new king of Newark.

I clenched my fist and gnawed my teeth in anger. "There will never be another CJ! What my brother did in this mutha-fuckin' city can't be duplicated. I promise y'all, before it's all said and done, I'ma do that bitch nigga, Nard, a thousand times worse than anyone can imagine."

"Death to his bitch ass!" said Premo. He held out his fist and I bumped it with mine. Snoop, Legend and the others followed suit.

I dried my eyes and looked around at the others. The pain that showed on their faces was as real as mine. CJ was like God in our eyes. Many people outside of our crew disliked him, but to those of us that he had love for, there wasn't a better nigga.

"Let's go in here and check on Rah, then we'll go to morgue to identify CJ's body," I said. I dreaded having to do that but it was inescapable.

We began to head back inside, moving as a unit. Suddenly, Snoop grabbed Shabazz by the collar and mugged him hard. "Hold up! How the fuck we know you're not down with the other side?" he questioned.

"I understand how you're feeling, yo. But you ain't gotta come at me like that. I didn't do nothin' to your mans, blood. If I could've helped them, I would've. But Nard and 'em were deep. They had choppaz and that pussy ass nigga, Nard, was using Rah as a shield. If I had clapped at him, I might've shot Rah by mistake. Even CJ couldn't do nothin'. He went out like a gangsta tho'. Wasn't no ho' in his blood. I'll forever remember that," said Shabazz.

"I hear you. But you haven't convinced me that you're not the enemy," spat Snoop. He eased his toolie out.

"Bruh, if it was like that Rah would've never made it out of there alive. They left him for dead. I'm the nigga that held his head in my lap so he wouldn't choke to death on his own blood.

"I didn't leave his side until I saw the flashing red and blues turn into the corner. And the only reason I left then was because I didn't want them jakes taking me down to the precinct and questioning me. I'm a street nigga. I don't talk to cops." His mouth was tight, as if he was insulted that his sincerity was being questioned.

I reached out and grabbed Snoop by the elbow, and led him a few feet away from the others, but he kept his stare fixed on Shabazz. His apprehension told me he was ready to murk dude.

"Fam, I think he's telling the truth. I see it in his eyes, and I can hear it in his voice," I said.

"Fuck that nigga, yo! I wanna nod him!"

I knew where my nigga was coming from, his grief over CJ's death made him want to clap *whoever*. I felt the same way but I was trying hard to keep my head. I placed my hand on his shoulder. "Stand down, my G. We're gonna make those niggaz pay. Shabazz ain't one of them though."

"You trust son, yo?"

"I don't trust no man that ain't broke bread or shed blood with me, but I believe what he told us. I've seen him around and from what I recall he don't rock with those niggaz. If I'm wrong, we'll bury him beside them."

Snoop nodded his head in agreement. He shoved his hands in his pockets and took a deep breath, letting it out slowly. "*Damn!* I can't believe this shit. CJ dead? Son, my head is all fucked up." Tears streaked down his face in the form of two rivers.

I gave him a long G-hug. "We're about to wipe out Nard's entire bloodline. That's on everything I love," I vowed.

"I'm ready to ride on him right now."

"I feel you, but let's go check on Rah first. Then we gotta handle things with CJ. After that, we gon' crush everybody connected to Nard."

"Real shit," he said with conviction.

We walked back over to where the others stood. "What's the verdict?" asked Premo.

I looked from him to Shabazz, whose eyes held no fear. "Homie good," I announced, dapping him up.

Shabazz' shoulders relaxed. "I appreciate that, son. You'll see, I'm official."

"You better be," I warned. I gave him a cold stare, exclamating my seriousness, and then we all walked back inside.

Available now on Amazon.

Acknowledgments

Wuz up! wuz up! wuz up! (In my Martin Lawrence Voice)

Yyyooooo can y'all believe that the Boss'N Up series is complete?! I can't. The feeling of completing a series is indescribable. Y'all just don't know how happy this made my heart.

Now with that being said, I'm going to be completely honest with you all. I literally started not to even do any acknowledgements bbuuuttt I couldn't end this series without sending out a special thanks to a few special people that's close to my heart. Sssoo let's kick these acknowledgements off!!!

First off let me send a HHHUUGGEEE S/O to GOD!!! You have blessed me to come so far in life, even when I was at my lowest point and didn't think I would make it! Thank you for all of the blessings that you choose to bestow upon me and my child's life!!!

To my beautiful Princess Neriah Krissett Dunlap!!!!! You just don't know how much Mommy loves you!!!! On my life I would go to was for you!!!! Just know everything mommy does is for you!!!!

To my momma "You know I, I, I love you! No matter what you do. Oh oh oh oh...."
Lol for though no lie that's the truth. Over the years we've had our ups and downs, but it has only made our bound that much closer. Thank you for being you and

everything you do. I also want to say I truly appreciate all the sacrifices that you made while raising me so that you could ensure that I had everything that I needed day in and day out. I will forever love you and respect you for that. Real talk!

To my siblings big ups love y'all. Hope you accomplish all of your goals in life.

I want to send a special shout out to my homies Sade, D, Jasmine, Ebonee C., Kay Kay,and Koren. Love y'all.

Big ups to my home skillet biscuit Courtney Banks. Thank you for being there for me when I barely had any one else to turn to. I truly appreciate it!!!

To Sher'Nee Love you lots bestie! Miss ya lots!

To Crystal I luh yuh gul!!!! Thanks for all you and grams help with Ri!

To Danyelle, Marquel, Shameer and Lalah!!! Y'all know y'all my boo's for life. Love y'all lots!!!

To Christa you know you like blood to me. Love you sis.

To my homie P. Kellz thanks for all of your kind words of encouragement and for being who you are. I wish all the success in the world to you. Y'all go check his music out on Itunes, Spotify hell everywhere Google him Lol. Watch out he about to blow!

To Forever Redd!!! Carolina's Stand Up!!!! Thank you for all of the love you have shown me and being one of my toughest critics when I slacked off bad on writing. Thank you. It helped get me back on the right track.

To Tranay Adams! Wuz good Killa!!!! Lol. His books though... check them out!!!

To all of LDP love y'all lots keep grinding!!!

To Misty!!! You can throw that damn skeleton away now!!! The book is finally out LOL. Y'all check her work out on Amazon!

To Destiny Skai!!!! Gggiirrrlll we in this bitch like swimwear Lol!!!! Y'all be sure to check her work out as well on Amazon!

To Kameelah THANK you for helping me out along with Destiny when it came to me trying to get up to Jersey to say Goodbye to my great grams!!!

To Miss. Erma!!! I love yoouuu!!!!

To Latisha!!!! You will forever be my boo Lol!!!!

I also wanna send out some love to the readers who have stuck with me over the years and never wavered no matter what. Daleisha Matthews, Jane Penella, Bernie Bagley, Sharon Bel, Helene Young, Kim TrueToMe LeBlanc, Slow Motion Gary, Rochelle Pettrie, Kim Tate, Me she and Nancy Pyram just to name a few. If I missed anyone charge my brain and now my heart. I'm writing this with a lot on my brain.

To the Sargents. Thank you all for being there at my lowest point well points rather, but especially last year. That was a tough time for me and something I will never forget. I love y'all more than you all will ever know!!!

To the HNIC CA$H.....I just wanna say Thank you for everything from giving me a shot not once but TWICE, and for being very patient with me over the years when it came to this series. I truly appreciate it.

Shout outs to the ladies of Let's Chat. Lissha Sadler and Toni Doe!!! Love y'all!!! Keep doing ya thing!!!

And last but not least shout out to my Grandma Marva, Grandma Davis, and Mommer. I miss you guys every day and wish you guys were here to see me grow even more as a young lady and to see me become the successful women you knew I could be. I LOVE Y'ALL. R.I.P!!!!

With that being said, I hope you all enjoyed my series!!! Stay tuned for more from ya girl!!!

Stay Connected with Us!

Text **LOCKDOWN** to 22828 to stay up-to-date with new releases, sneak peaks, contests and more…

<u>Coming Soon from Lock Down Publications/Ca$h Presents</u>

BOW DOWN TO MY GANGSTA

By **Ca$h & Jamaica**

TORN BETWEEN TWO

By **Coffee**

CUM FOR ME **IV**

By **Ca$h & Company**

BLOOD OF A BOSS **IV**

By **Askari**

BRIDE OF A HUSTLA **III**

THE FETTI GIRLS

By **Destiny Skai**

WHEN A GOOD GIRL GOES BAD **II**

By **Adrienne**

LOVE & CHASIN' PAPER **II**

By **Qay Crockett**

THE HEART OF A GANGSTA **II**

By **Jerry Jackson**

TO DIE IN VAIN **II**

By **ASAD**

THE BOSS MAN'S DAUGHTERS **III**

BAE BELONGS TO ME **II**

By **Aryanna**

A DOPEBOY'S PRAYER **II**

By **Eddie "Wolf" Lee**

Available Now

(CLICK TO PURCHASE)

RESTRAING ORDER **I & II**

By **CA$H & Coffee**

LOVE KNOWS NO BOUNDARIES **I II & III**

By **Coffee**

LAY IT DOWN **I & II**

LAST OF A DYING BREED

By **Jamaica**

PUSH IT TO THE LIMIT

By **Bre' Hayes**

BLOOD OF A BOSS **I II & III**

By **Askari**

THE STREETS BLEED MURDER **I, II & III**

THE HEART OF A GANGSTA

By **Jerry Jackson**

CUM FOR ME

CUM FOR ME 2

An **LDP Erotica Collaboration**

BRIDE OF A HUSTLA **I & II**

By **Destiny Skai**

WHEN A GOOD GIRL GOES BAD

By **Adrienne**

A GANGSTER'S REVENGE **I II III & IV**

THE BOSS MAN'S DAUGHTERS

THE BOSS MAN'S DAUGHTERS **II**

A SAVAGE LOVE **I & II**

By **Aryanna**

A DOPEBOY'S PRAYER

By **Eddie "Wolf" Lee**

WHAT ABOUT US **I & II**

NEVER LOVE AGAIN

THUG ADDICTION

By **Kim Kaye**

THE KING CARTEL **I, II & III**

By **Frank Gresham**

THESE NIGGAS AIN'T LOYAL **I, II & III**

By **Nikki Tee**

GANGSTA SHYT **I II &III**

By **CATO**

THE ULTIMATE BETRAYAL

By **Phoenix**

DON'T FU#K WITH MY HEART **I & II**

By **Linnea**

I LOVE YOU TO DEATH

By Destiny J

I RIDE FOR MY HITTA

I STILL RIDE FOR MY HITTA

By **Misty Holt**

LOVE & CHASIN' PAPER

By **Qay Crockett**

TO DIE IN VAIN

By **ASAD**

HEARTLESS THUGS

By **Royal Nicole**

BOOKS BY LDP'S CEO, CA$H

(CLICK TO PURCHASE)

TRUST IN NO MAN

TRUST IN NO MAN 2

TRUST IN NO MAN 3

BONDED BY BLOOD

SHORTY GOT A THUG

THUGS CRY

THUGS CRY 2

THUGS CRY 3

TRUST NO BITCH

TRUST NO BITCH 2

TRUST NO BITCH 3

TIL MY CASKET DROPS

RESTRAINING ORDER

RESTRAINING ORDER 2

IN LOVE WITH A CONVICT

Coming Soon

BONDED BY BLOOD 2

BOW DOWN TO MY GANGSTA

Boss'N Up 3

Printed in the USA
CPSIA information can be obtained
at www.ICGtesting.com
LVHW080953031123
762978LV00014B/163

9 781548 664800